SONGS IN A BOX

Book Two from Stories in Glass

Paul S. Moore

Cover design copyright © 2020 by Niki Lenhart
nikilen-designs.com

Published by Water Dragon Publishing

waterdragonpublishing.com

ISBN 978-1-946907-01-1 (Trade Paperback)

FIRST EDITION

10 9 8 7 6 5 4 3 2 1

PROLOGUE

THE AFTERMATH

C HRISTMAS AT THE BILL ELLIOTT COMPOUND on Kensington Ave. was a gloomy event in 2005. Po, heavy with child, wanted to be in the company of those adventurers who could understand her worries. She invited Asitr's old crew for Christmas dinner. Only Lock and Hayak accepted her invitation.

Lockjaw showed up drunk and passed out before dinner.

Over a bowl of warm, buttered-rum bread pudding, Po told Hayak, "I'll stay here until Bobby returns. He won't be abandoned. Even if he returns infected with Kuru."

Hayak ended the evening with a confession. "I am not a creepy man, but I watch. I have been struck by love at first surveillance. I am here for whatever you need."

*　　*　　*

Christmas, 2006 saw Hayak and Po Asmudi celebrate the season as man and wife.

Po couldn't fully embrace happy. Little things, fleeting fears, premonitions, didn't allow the full cup. A Christmas card addressed to Lockjaw, and returned as undeliverable, brought sudden tears.

Behind her, at the tree, her family brought her back to happy thoughts. Hayak, holding tiny Roberta up to the tree so she could touch the lights, began to sing. "*Fa la la la la.*"

"Ba ba ba ba ba," came the adorable, chortling reply.

"Come, be with us," Hayak called.

As Po turned, he saw tears in her eyes. "Oh, you cry. Please tell us which eye spills the unhappy tears. Only those will I dry."

"*Fa la la,* baby. Best Christmas ever." She smiled the smile of contentment.

1

O TIS BECKLEY LOOKED TOWARD THE WINDOW in his room and pointed. "It's been dark outside for a while. Do you appreciate it? Night and day, our clock before we had clocks." Otis huffed a quick breath. "You don't know what it's like to be without something to measure time."

"I didn't appreciate the passage of time until our first Christmas in the box. That marker on the calendar helped us to reconnect with the sense of normalcy we had lost. For Bobby, it was one step away from a dark abyss.

"Although Bobby, when snared, was the first of us in the box to speak, he fell silent. Stone cold silent. We worried about him. We Cajoled him, tossed platitudes at him, even tried the double-dog-dare-you. Bobby's retreat into his sanctuary of silence endured. In the box, we had a sense ... a sure feeling, that Bobby's spirit was sick and dying."

Otis stared toward the ceiling, but his focus was set on something very far away. "When we witnessed an event in a far corner of the Milky Way, things changed for us. Asitr and I began thinking about the passage of time. Bobby allowed the door to his fortress of solitude to open, just a crack. The inciting event was an angelic celebration of Christmas."

Otis paused, and when he spoke again, he spoke in tones of wonder. "The stars set the stage. They focused like tiny spotlights, each beam directing their unique white blend of colors onto floating particles of dust. Each tiny particle reflected and refracted the lights until a waving display of soft colors enveloped a choir of swaying shapes. The detail of the figures in the choir were as elusive to the eye as sculptures made of glass. These transparent angels hummed melodies to make Hoagy Carmichael burn his collective works. When lyrics were added, harmonies enriched the wonder.

"Coordinated motion, undulating within the colors, moved in perfect sync with the rhythm of the music on the dramatic stage. When the last note hung in the air, the forms of the choir melded into the curtain of wavy light, and slowly turned from softly bright to deeply luxurious. While voices faded, one baritone note remained. The curtain waved like the Northern Lights, in a deep blend of burgundy and maroon, then it dropped away as the single voice went silent, returning the star's lights to their normal, individual duties and the dust to its wandering.

"When the music stopped, Bobby summed the scene with a word from the first language, 'O'. The closest translation in English would be 'WOW'."

Otis sighed deeply. Worry lines etched his face. "It would be another year, to the day, before Bobby spoke again."

Before continuing, Otis poured a glass of water and sipped it slowly. "Tick Tock, Tick Tock," he said, and waited until he drained his glass to continue.

"We pleaded with Kae'Lairy for some way to mark time in the box. He was as silent as Bobby, but accidentally, a breakthrough happened. In the old tongue, Asitr, responded to Kae'Lairy's silence in aggravation, 'I might as well be talking to the walls.'

"Voila. The walls responded with a tone like a tap of a wooden spoon against an iron skillet. The box, we discovered, was responsive to the old language. We asked for a calendar and one appeared. 'Well, deck the walls,' Asitr said. 'Happy New Year.'

"I asked for hot chocolate and a candy cane. We learned the walls had sensible limits.

"Our first calendar displayed the mechanics of Heaven's cycles, but soon, with a little dialogue and mathematical tinkering, we had a calendar set to the measuring of years, as defined by the rate of the earth's race around our sun, and a clock set to the hours and length of days, as measured by the home planet's rate of spin.

"When December rolled around again, we were weary of passing time as space tourists on a runaway bus." Otis huffed a chuckle and grinned broadly. "You know that anticipation for the coming of Christmas isn't just a kid thing. I had the Santa's-on-his-way feeling as Christmas approached in 2006. Our spirits, and this is an accurate description, Doc, our spirits vibrated in anticipation. We anticipated the euphoria of another magical concert. What we got, instead, was the solo voice of Kae'Lairy, wailing as we sped away to the debris field of the planet Tiamat.

"Asitr was right. Nothing prepares you for the effects of an angel's wail. Our spirits knotted like the painful cramping of muscle.

"Even in our discomfort, we understood. Ka'Lairy was reacting to the cancellation of our appearance at the concert. It was clear. Our captor was shunned by his kind, and broken.

"Asitr asked, rhetorically. 'Is this a good thing?'

"I didn't have a response, but Bobby had something to say to our broken angel. 'Now you're sorry aren't you, you mighty bag of poop. Take me home, now. I have to see my wife and child.' "We had our Christmas words from Bobby McKinney. Immediately after his outburst, he returned to silence.

"From Kae'Lairy, we received a Christmas gift. On the wall, between the calendar and the clock, was evidence of what Kae'Lairy was searching for in the debris field. A screen appeared with the opening logo for the game of Asteroids. Asitr wasn't interested, but I tried to enjoy the gift. I figured out how to play without benefit of nervous fingers jumping from button to button. I willed, by thought, the endangered little spaceship through the hurtling asteroids, never in danger of crashing. If I continued to play, my high score would be infinity. Boring, pointless infinity. '*Fa la la la la.* Most depressing Christmas ever,' I said.

"Asitr added to the gloom. "I bet Lock is having a rough go of things, too."

2

LOCKJAW'S YEAR OF BREAKING APART

ASITR HAD REASON TO WORRY. Lock wasn't coping well on earth. He was lonely, disappointed, depressed, bitter, and angry.

His 2005 New Year Resolution was to get his balance back and find a place, a cause, a group, a person to connect with. He wanted his sense of purpose back. To that end, he threw his golden calf into the boot of his Range Rover and drove. He was *Uneasy Rider*, looking for America. When his journey ended, he was lonely, disappointed, depressed, bitter, angry, and, most of the time, drunk.

On New Year's Eve of 2006, he was on a plane to Panama, sitting in a window seat, fighting an obsessive loop of self-pitying thoughts. The loop began to mercifully unravel after a bright-eyed woman nestled next to him in the aisle seat. After perfunctory greetings, the woman asked, "So, how did you find yourself heading off to Panama for the New Year?"

"Just traveling. Looking."

"And what have you found, so far?"

Locks answer boiled out of him like blood, and diarrhea from an Ebola victim. The dam burst.

"I found my country is made up of zombie tribes."

"Zombie tribes?" The woman turned in her seat to face him.

"Tribes of white-collar thralls, enablers, tied to their eugenic masters, paving the golden road to control, and congratulating each other for their bogus ascendancy into the clique of *Masters of the Universe.*"

"Yeah?"

"I found lawyers sipping artificially-colored water and alcohol in tiny glasses. Every one of them up to their fifty-dollar socks in shallow shit and acting like they're swimming in a private Tahitian lagoon."

"That's funny."

"I found robots, programmed to maximize profit algorithms, without regard for the future of the next generations, doomed to be born in the deep end of the shit pool, opportunity for success reduced to accidents of birth."

"My, that's ..."

"I found night clubs where hip-hop gangsters welcomed me as an out-of-style *niggah* who needed some bling lessons, a line of coke with a Courvoisier chaser, and a paid hour with a cold *ho.*"

"Hmm."

"I found neighborhoods where the bright lights fade into the off and on glow of dim street lamps, where *hard niggahs* lurk to hustle their way to funding their promotion into the Courvoisier and coke club. Remorseless soul brothers, with no respect for souls, pants down below their asses, demanding respect. Their community enablers, monopolizing the camera lights of pandering news networks, always blaming white racism, white cops, and not-black-enough independent thinkers for every problem in their culture. They demand a dialogue about race with one breath and damn differing opinions with the dismissive word, *racist*, in the next."

"Yes, that's a ..."

"I found dying rural communities and rotting suburban neighborhoods where white tribes, who've forgotten their traditional principles have lost the definition of conservative, liberal, and common good."

"It's all so ..."

"I discovered dumbed-down generations unable to see their *trickle-down* economy is written on sponges to absorb every stray nickel generated by labor. Even sheep know if their living pasture is sold as sod and replaced by dead straw. White folks with a little money? They invest in the sod companies."

"I think ..."

"In the tribes where skin color doesn't define a person's belief system, I saw people marching in parades, insisting the public display of their sexual preferences is a civil rights issue."

"But ..."

"I found an educational system snuffing out the curiosity of children who want to explore evidence of an intelligent design in the world around them. Their questions mocked as ridiculous superstition."

"So sad."

"I found the toolbox where phonics is replaced by lists of words to be memorized. Human history is taught without the flesh of the ideas that molded the famous names to rethink and drive themselves to initiate the human events."

"It's so ..."

"Don't get me started on cable news. They inflame the splintered parts of my country and ridicule anyone outside their circle of spin who yells fire.

"I learned, when hate is oxygen, reason is kindling. I found out I don't have a fire hose."

"You can't ..."

"I found the only gathering of the tribes takes place in voting booths, where the outcome is always the same. 'You have to vote for a demolican or republicrat,' they say. 'It's stupid to waste your vote.' Waste? Keep doing it the same way, expecting different outcomes is the definition of insanity, I say."

"Yes."

"What about you? Would you rather be stupid or crazy?"

"If I ..."

"Worst of all, I found out God allows devils to steal infants and use them in the most horrific acts of depravity, for the pleasure of inhaling the emotions of innocent terror ... I ... I should stop. I guess I've been away too long and preoccupied with ... Never mind. Tell me, what have you found?"

The woman slowly stood, still smiling, and answered, "Okay, look, I've found a window seat. You have a good new year, sir."

As she walked down the aisle of the plane, Lock looked out the window and onto the tarmac, thinking, *Damn, I've gone mad ...Or have I?*

3

NEW YEAR IN PANAMA — 2007
REBOOTING MR. SMITH

L OCK WOKE UP TOO LATE FOR LUNCH and reached for the rum
bottle by the bed. It was empty, so he rolled over and tried to
sleep again, but the bright Panama sun shot through the balcony
door in straight lines between the slats. He felt like he was being
scanned by a giant barcode device. The light hurt his eyes, but he
couldn't move his head to avoid it unless he turned toward the
wall with the annoying photo display.

In Lock's year of traveling, he learned one thing: Sit up slowly
after a night of heavy drinking.

When he let his feet find the floor, he moved them around to
find his sandals. When he couldn't locate them by touch, he
opened his eyes and looked down, finding he still had his shoes on.
Across the room, he spotted his unpacked bag on the dresser.
Sitting atop his bag were his sunglasses.

After making the distance to his bag, Lock put the sunglasses
over his eyes and looked around the room thinking, for just a

moment, he might be in Viet Nam again. The furniture was bamboo and rattan. Mosquito netting, draped above the bed, ready to be unfurled with a tug of a string, brought back memories of the tropical world where he once shot his Grampy.

After his eyes settled on the wall of photographs over the dresser, he confirmed he was in Panama. The odd photo collection, Monkey Fist plants, an aerial photo of dozens of scattered, tiny islands, a modern photo of Chinese engineers at the canal, and an old photo, one of dozens publicly displayed by Manuel Noriega for the news media. The photo, made public two weeks before the U.S. Invasion of Panama, showed CIA director George Bush the senior, sharing pizza with Noriega on a couch in the dictator's home.

It was the last photo that brought Lock's mind back to similarities between Panama and Viet Nam again. He swiped at the irritating photo with his hand to knock it from the wall, but only managed to partially tear away his middle fingernail. The photo was securely screwed in place.

He hopped backward, grimacing, finger in mouth, until he stumbled against the slatted door to his balcony. "There's a bar on the beach," he said aloud, then opened the door and walked to the railing, in hopes of spotting it.

His ears followed the sound of music, and there it was: small tables with blue and white parasols angled toward the sun, arranged in a semi-circle around a palm thatched tiki hut. In the crowd of tourists in bathing suits, all sitting with their back to the hotel and facing the ocean, one figure stood out by being different. Sitting with her body in shade, but with the sun falling on an open book in her hands, was a dark-skinned woman in a white cotton dress. He couldn't see her face clearly, but he knew it was her: the woman from the airplane.

A shower, an apology, and an offer to buy dinner became the plan.

When Lock finished cleaning up, he headed for the tiki bar, but the woman was no longer there. He looked for her in a crowd of people standing on the beach, but he didn't see her. As more and more people — tourist and local — turned the crowd into a throng,

Lock grew curious about what they were gathered for, so he walked onto the beach and joined them.

Soon, the reason for the gathering was obvious. The sun was falling. At the end of the world, the sun burned orange as it sped its departure from the day and plunged into the ocean. When the last hot sliver disappeared, leaving colorful clouds above and a darkened ocean below, the crowd erupted in cheers, whistles, and applause. Sparked by the continuation of island music at the tiki bar, dancing on the beach greeted a new cycle of life on one sandy acre of the world. In the center of it, he spotted her, swaying gracefully, dancing alone, and smiling.

Lock waited for the song to end before he tapped her on the shoulder. "Hi there, don't be afraid, I want to apologize," he said. "I'd like to ask you to dinner and chat."

She didn't answer right away, but she wasn't timid. "I'll let you buy me a rum runner, on ice, not frozen, if you let me buy you a Shirley Temple, umbrella optional."

Taken a little aback by the proviso, Lock attempted a defense. "I'm not an alcoholic, just an angry fool."

"Good, then you won't mind going without alcohol for a night. I'm Willa Vernon, and you are?"

"I am ... I'm John Smith. I would love to glean the secrets of happiness from you over dinner and wine. I might be a troubled spirit, but I'm no Shirley Temple."

"Okay, Mr. John Smith, I think you should know you had me at 'zombie tribes', but lost me at 'devils inhaling baby terror'. Do you have a good local place to recommend, or should we eat the tourist fare?"

4

NEW YEAR'S RESOLUTIONS IN A BOX — 2007

THE NEW YEAR WITH THE LUCKY NUMBER SEVEN at the end started differently than the past year. Bobby was less and less in our thoughts. Figuring out Kae'Lairy was turning into a guessing game with fewer than a dozen questions, continually asked, and never answered.

Asitr set a new chain in motion when he asked me, "Can you convert the *Asteroid* computer to different tasks?"

I wasn't bragging. Back on earth, I'd already managed to use the old binary language to convert the PCs and internet servers to spoken command. "I'll have a working blank tablet by tomorrow. Then we can figure out what we want it to do."

"Same problems, different approach," Asitr said. "I don't have anything actionable in mind. I'm thinking about Lock and Dave, when they sat at a campfire in *Eden,* asking round questions with square answers. Maybe a computer will help round out the holes or square up some questions."

I don't think Asitr was computer savvy enough to realize a computer needed to be fed answers first, then asked questions second. I understood the computer as a back-engineered brain, without the ability to conjure questions by wondering what, where, or why. *Grok*-ing the difference was my moment of understanding the chicken/egg design. I didn't tell Asitr the project would lead us to dead loops, and I didn't share my personal epiphany. To each his own moment. Enoch had his stone. Asitr had his download of lives. I had my understanding of a computer. Bobby... well, what would Bobby have? I took on the project as boredom therapy. As it turned out, it was therapy for Bobby, as well.

"Leave room for sound recording." It wasn't Christmas, but Bobby McKinney, spoke. Then, once again, silence.

As promised, I had a working blank tablet in less than twenty-four hours. It was April on earth before I managed to cut out some space for sound recording. It was the first day of April to be exact. A date Bobby brought to our attention.

"I don't believe you," he said. "It's just a big ha-ha April fool's joke on stupid old Bobby McKinney." At least we knew he was paying attention to the calendar.

I don't know if Asitr was fed up, recognized Bobby's regression, or stumbled on the magic button. He took off the kid gloves. "*Nana nana na na*," he said, taunting the man-child with a devastating volley of kindergarten argument. "Bobby's getting laughed at. Bobby's getting laughed at."

Bobby was quick in his response. "Ass-eater, Ass-eater, has a funny na-ame."

If Asitr had pushed the magic button to open Bobby up, I want to take credit for the timely verbal pushing of the record button. "Bik," I said quietly into the machine, just before the exchange, then I spoke the command to play back what I recorded. "Bok."

The tiny speakers replayed the taunting rudeness of a playground argument. The tinny voices echoed in the box. The echo stopped, then everything went quiet again. For maybe five seconds.

First Asitr, then Bobby, then I started to laugh. "What did you call me?" Asitr laughed through the question. "If you had a face, I'd wash your mouth out with soap."

Laughing, Bobby responded, "*Nyuk, nyuk, nyuk,* funny man."

Playground diplomacy. In the big world, the language is more eloquent, but the message is the same. Sometimes, it brings peace. In the small world of the box, laughter, the first laugh in our tour of the universe, was medicine. Bobby emerged from his dark hole, and the three of us found ourselves on the same page, trying to figure out why we were here.

Bobby had a suggestion for where to start. "Let's make a list of everything we have in common. We can call it our one-hundred percent list."

Agreeing on the obvious went quickly. We were male. We all were capable of speaking the old language. We didn't know why we were here.

Bobby offered another item for the list. "Alayat," he said, "We all know Alayat. He's one of us. An innocent victim of the angel, Kae'Lairy."

Asitr and I understood he wasn't privy to the photos from the fax machine. Neither of us wanted to send him back into hiding.

"Robert," Asitr said, "I'm going to call you 'Robert' while we're working together as team-mates. When you run and hide, I'm going to call you 'Bobby'. Don't feel like I'm shaming you. I just believe I have to distinguish between the little boy who's earned every bit of anger in him, and the amazing man who refuses to quit.

"I had a Savant friend named Quetzacatl. He saw the barrier vines protecting the Savant tribe as a cage constraining his curiosity. Quetzacatl needed to get out, but ...

"I know about Quetz, Asitr. Are you going to tell me I'm some sort of show-offy snake-bird?"

"Sheesh, Bobby."

"Sheesh natso. Call me Robert."

"What I'm trying to say is this. Whatever news you take to heart, good or bad ..."

"I see, Asitr, don't finish. You're going to tell me something you think is going to make me crazy and you don't want me to hide. You want me to be like Quetz and find a hole to dive in, hoping I'll pop out the other side."

"Well, no, but yes. I was trying to boost you up for bad news."

"How about just giving me the facts."

"I'll give you some bad news straight out, Robert. Just the conclusion, not the facts. Alayat is the vilest spirit imaginable. I won't entertain any argument to the contrary. Don't ask me what I know. You can see for yourself when we get out of here. I insist we don't argue about Alayat. The One-Hundred Percent Club is a group of three."

"Fair enough, dipnot. Let's find our rabbit hole."

5

PINEAPPLES IN PANAMA

W HEN WILLA ACCEPTED THE INVITATION TO DINNER, Lock asked her one question: "Do you prefer predictably good or sometimes spectacular, with a chance of whipped cream and baloney over egg noodles in tartar sauce?"

"I don't believe in predictably good." she said. "I do believe in adventure with back-up plans. Is there a good pizza joint near the restaurant?"

The adventurous spirit paid off. Pineapple Sam was available for the next evening. When his guest list of two showed up, he was on his quirky game.

At the center of Sam's property, elevated five feet above the terrain, sat a patio with an overarching lattice of hand-woven jungle vines, several large brick ovens topped with a wizard's variety of smoking charcoal pits, and a single table for dining.

To make their way to the seating under the vine lattice, the diners walked a twisting path through a maze of pineapple beds. Halfway to the patio, an aroma overwhelmed them. Lock and Willa both tilted their heads upward and inhaled, eyes closed, toes curled, and taste buds jumping to attention.

Before any eating could begin, Sam had to read the rules. "If you want a menu, they are on sale at the gift shop at the bottom of the compost pile," he said. "We have a full stock of menus from the most common burger doodle restaurants and one rare reprint of a vintage *Burger Chef* menu. We don't use menus. We don't do appetizers. We serve four courses. I call them breakfast, lunch, dinner, and dessert. We never know what we are going to make until it's finished. We follow our nose. We don't measure, and we don't have recipes. If you don't finish your breakfast, you skip lunch. If you're too slow in finishing your breakfast, night descends. No lunch will be served after dark. No substitutions, no boogers under the table, and no refunds."

Willa was laughing through her hands when the rules were read. "I think he's serious, John. Let's hurry up and agree so we don't miss lunch."

Breakfast was a small misshapen omelet of egg, horseradish, sharp cheddar, and minced celery, seared in bacon grease, but still crisp. The chaser was freshly-made mango and pomegranate juice.

The meal was devoured with loud *mmm*s, and lunch was served in time to see the late light of the evening rest on the butterfly garden at the ridge line in the west. At Pineapple Sam's oasis, the sun called it a day with a burst of flittering, flashing wings, like a rear guard for the sun, batting the last stray lumens into the advancing darkness.

A comfortable silence, shared through brief glances, allowed the salmon-colored sky to take its sweet time performing shift-changing theater for the silent audience. It was perfect for both of them. Each one needed the moment for reasons the other couldn't share.

John and Willa didn't really know each other, but they were comfortable together. By the time the lunch course came, they knew silence didn't have to be awkward on a first date. Soon after Sam brought glasses of milk, plates of warm cashew-buttered toast, crisp and sticky yogurt-glazed yam fries, and apple wedges, they began to share a little of themselves.

Lock told her he was retired from the importing business, recently got his helicopter license, and was in Panama to pick up his first flying machine.

Willa told Lock she was a retired anthropologist, freed from her labors by frugal living, and an even more frugal aunt, now deceased, who remembered her in her will.

While waiting for the main course, they began fleshing out their biographies.

Lock began peeling the onion of his background when Willa asked him why he wanted a helicopter. "I want to leave my grandfather's ashes with a tribe we met a long time ago," he said. "I'm too old to go on foot."

"Oh, you must be excited. A last travel adventure," Willa gushed, "I'm happy for you."

"He had enough of the short life and wanted to go home."

"That's comforting ... the short life. I hope he didn't suffer."

"He suffered often." The answer wasn't what Lockjaw wanted to say. He was enjoying a peaceful evening, and didn't mean to open any doors to his *Twilight Zone* past. Reversing the field, he added, "Grampy had plenty of good times. You would've liked him. How about you? How did your journeys bring you here?"

"I'm here to finish a project I started for my Doctoral thesis. The project jumpstarted my career, but I never finished it. You know what Doctor Who says: *'First things first, but not in that order.'* Gotta listen to the Doctor."

"What's your topic?" Lock preferred asking questions to answering them, so he kept them coming. "How did your paper start your career?"

"Quetzacatl," she said. "His metamorphosis from minor god among gods to god of gods. From flying feathered serpent, to bearded man with a prickly crown, buried face down so he could descend into the underworld, defeat the dark gods, and return to bring victory to man. I was working on the timelines of his changes, comparing his evolution to world events in the same time frame."

"Interesting. Have you formulated a theory? Was it the project or the quality of research that got you noticed?"

"Yes," Willa laughed at the rapid-fire questions. "My professor knew of some similar research by a Stanford team and, yes, they liked how I prepared the work. No, to the other. The theory is still in the gathering of reference-points stage."

"Years of working with a professional team didn't help pull it together?"

"No, I never had time to revisit ol' snake feathers while I was working. Quetz and I have a date that's been a long time coming. I'm in Panama to research some local libraries for items mentioned in the corporate collections."

"Are you getting any help from your old employers?"

"My old employers aren't interested in Quetzacatl. They wanted my methodology. Their goal was to find anthropological events preceding large cultural shifts. They wanted to catalog action/reaction events throughout history that have near one-hundred percent predictability. In the end, they kept pushing for dates and events related to the Mayan calendar."

"What did they do with your work?"

"They claimed it as their intellectual property. Quetz is the only thing left I can call my own. They never directed me to write up a report on him."

"No more corporate anthropology for you?" Lock asked the question and leaned away from the sizzling sound getting closer to his right ear.

Sam pushed between them, interrupting their eye contact, and laid a sizzling iron plate onto a teak block in front of Willa. Her nostrils flared when the smoky steam rose to her face.

"Quetzacatl's all mine," Willa said, while reaching for her fork.

Lock was still leaning into Willa's plate when he heard a thump announcing the arrival of his own sizzling plate of chicken breast.

"Par-boiled in rum," announced Sam. "Marinated in buttered vinegar, covered with a blend of freshly roasted and chopped peppers, baked under coals in a banana leaf wrap, then smothered in a thick sauce of instant coffee, coarse peppercorns, molasses, cocoa, and lime. Finally, flash broiled to glaze the sauce. A bowl of goat cream with mint, basil, cilantro, and pear juice, poured over cucumber, is for coating the tongue between pepper burn surprises. Enjoy."

Throughout the main course, conversation turned into a session of short questions and short answers, each question asked while the brain was cycling between curiosity and food intoxication. The answers, given between bites, were more like sound effects than words.

As each of them wiped their mouths at the end of the course, they realized there were no more safe questions or safe answers left. Along with the meal, Lock and Willa had eaten through the tough outer layers of their personal onions. Only the soft, delicate center was left a mystery.

For Willa, the big question about the inner layer of John Smith's onion boiled down to wanting to know which man she was dining with. Was he an adventurous world traveler, sincere in both rant and regret? Is he an angry man by nature? Could he be a spook, sent to keep her aware she was being monitored?

Lock didn't have paranoid ideas concerning Willa's intentions. He had doubts about his own layers.

How did he get to the point where he had to start watching what he said? Why did he want to tell her what was at the center of his onion? Why did he feel she would run away if he did? How did he get to this point so quickly with a woman he knew for only two days?

Willa broke the silence with a purposeful question. "Why were you so on edge at the airport?"

Lock tried to answer openly, without the details. "I was wound too tight," he said. "In two years, I went from feeling bullet-proof to bullet-riddled. I was confident I was part of something important, and sure of success. Then, in one night, I lost my faith. I lost my rock. My grandfather died suddenly and, when he went, my big important project went with him. After that, a vacuum. A purposeless vacuum. So, I tried to reacquaint myself with my country. That didn't work out so well either. Traveling around, looking for a place to settle, I felt like an astronaut, all set to de-orbit, just as his planet blows up. My options felt limited to trying a trip of light years distance on a tank with eight hours of air, or sending a farewell message to a dead planet, *'Houston, you have a problem'*. I don't understand how any of it happened so fast."

"The old question." Willa said the words as if she were using them to jog her memory. "Can we keep our lives as we know them? Something like that ..."

"Hmm?" Lock wiped his mouth again and drummed his fingers on the table.

"Willa followed up with Olphrenjii's response to Auth when he asked the same question at the Bombag campfire. "None do."

Suddenly, paranoia jumped to Lock's side of the table. "That's very interesting," he said.

"Just something from a radio play I heard. I've had it on my mind the last couple of days."

"Oh? Interesting."

"I remembered the show after we got off the plane. I was watching you get your luggage at the carousel and worrying you were going batty for all the right reasons. There was a character in the play with a good answer for how to deal with situations when anger is justified but nothing can be done. He said he wanted to howl at the moon, couldn't change it, and won't accept it. Sure, it's obtuse advice, but it's a three-legged stool that helped me balance my own anger issues at the time I heard the show."

"Hmm. Interesting. He sounds like an admirable fellow."

Willa went on. "Just a character in a play. He had a name like a disease. Anthrax, rabies, something like that. He also referred to — or maybe another character referred to — our own time on the planet with the same phrase you use. 'The short life.' Small sentence; big meaning."

Lock searched his memory for other things he may have said.

Willa rambled. "You must think I have a lame philosophy. Do your time, do your best, and don't expect success. Anyway, not to change the subject, but I wonder what dessert will be."

"Here at Pineapple Sam's, some things never change. Dessert will be ..."

Across from where his guests were sitting, Pineapple Sam made a startling, sudden appearance announced by the loud bang of a machete handle striking the table. "It's time to lop off a head and give it a haircut," he said. "Papa's going hunting. Are you ready?"

"Just do it, Papa Pineapple," Lock said, "Let's end this thing."

Willa, startled by the loud interruption, jerked both hands up to her throat and stiffened. "Just do what?" she asked. "Do what?"

Lock put a hand on her shoulder, laughing. "You should go with him. See a good nose in action. Dessert here is always the same. Tell her why, Sam."

"Because, the magnificent aroma and flavor of a pineapple, picked and eaten at its golden peak, can make all things right. Nothing added. All its qualities brought to the table at the moment of their zenith and devoured in their moment of glory. Hallelujah."

"Sam likes pineapples." Lock said with a straight face. "He really likes pineapples."

"I like 'em at their peak," he replied. "I like the way they let you know it's their time. If you follow me, while I follow my nose, you can see why you're getting yours with a haircut. Are you both coming? I need someone to hold the flashlight."

"If the lady will join me." Lock offered his hand.

Willa accepted. "Who could pass up the rare opportunity of watching a nosy man give haircuts to pineapples?"

Sam passed his flashlight to Lock and bowed, speaking in a theatrical voice. "Mr. Lockjaw? If you will shed some light, the lady and I will stroll." He turned to the stairs leading down from the patio, bent forward, holding his machete with both hands behind his back. Making his guests scramble to keep up, he took off in a Groucho Marx walk through the pineapple beds, sniffing as he went.

Walking in shadows behind Lock, Willa felt pushed from behind by the dark and pulled forward by the light, her mind locked into a mystery. The mystery was spawned by a certainty, newly learned when Sam addressed John Smith. The man with a disease for a name, her memory reminded her, was John *'Lockjaw'* Smith.

Pushed by the dark, pulled by the light, indeed.

Her fight or flight was stuck in neutral, so she followed, chasing in shadow, wondering if it was really going to be a pineapple receiving a haircut for its disembodied head, and hopeful the path would lead to enlightenment. Because she believed in adventure with a back-up plan, she brought her steak knife along.

"Aha. I found you." Sam stopped moving and his machete caught the light, pointing at a golden pineapple. Lock held the flashlight steady on the target, and the machete fell with a whoosh, leaving Sam holding the severed fruit by the green leaves atop its dome. Sam carried his prize a few steps into the pineapple bed and stopped, kicking at the dirt in a gap between plants. "Your new home," he said, as he sawed the stiff leaves from the fruit. Next, he set the leaves on top of the dirt and said, "It is finished. It is begun. Hallelujah."

Turning around to make their way back through the maze to their table, Willa was in the lead, taking her eyes from the path only when she noticed a moving light. "Who is that on the patio?"

"That would be Shori, the wife," Sam said. "Choosing the wine, clearing the dishes, counting the silverware, bringing the go-box for the pineapple, and checking for boogers under the table."

"Oh, we're taking the pineapple home?" Willa moved a little quicker, hoping she could add her steak knife to the inventory before it was counted as missing.

"We didn't have a wine to go with your meal, so you have to take a bottle home. The pineapple should be eaten on the beach. Tonight. I mean that. Eat it tonight. I don't care which beach, as long as you're comfortable. This pineapple requires the proper setting, and all your attention. It's the rules."

On a nearly silent drive back to the Hotel beach, Willa asked a question of real importance to her. "God's truth, John, who are you?"

6

MOST FIRST DATES DON'T END with one of the parties giving instructions for how best to make sure the other was successful in murdering them, but ...

"I'm not Ted Kaczynski," Willa sliced the last piece of pineapple from the core, and walked into the water to wash the stickiness from her hands. When she returned to her lounger, she scraped the carcass of the fruit into the bag and said her good-nights. "Please," she said, "don't bother seeing me to the door."

Walking ten feet away to drop the bag in the trash receptacle, she left Lock with her piece of advice. "I'm having room-service breakfast tomorrow. If you want me to have a heart attack, don't poison the orange juice. I don't always finish my orange juice. Poison the eggs. I always finish my eggs. I promise you, if the torture continues, I'll do what they're afraid I'll do."

Watching Willa walk back to the hotel, Lock wrung his hands and whispered his disappointment to his old, departed confidant.

"Crap, Grampy, who said the truth will set you free? Kicked to the Curb is more like it."

*   *   *

In the morning, Lock intercepted the man delivering Willa's breakfast, tipped him, then placed an unbound manuscript on the tray, along with a CD player loaded with a recording of Asitr's appearances on Bill Elliot's show. The manuscript came with a bookmark placed at a story not told on the air. On the bookmark was a scribbled note:

> *I hope this helps your research for Quetzacatl. I know you're not the Unabomber.*
> *I'm not Dr. Henry Murray. It's safe to eat the eggs. I'm leaving after check-out on Monday. If you prefer not to talk, please leave the book at the desk.*

Early Monday morning, Lock loaded his most precious cargo into the helicopter. His checklist included Asitr's ashes, a bag of seeds, a well-travelled guitar, and a heavy golden idol with etchings on its forehead. He covered them with one suitcase and camping supplies. Two more items remained on his wish list. The book of Asitr's stories to the Savant and his only invited guest. He trusted the book would be at the desk before checkout time, but he doubted she would make the trip. It was, after all, an adventure with no back-up plan.

After turning on the hangar security system and locking the door, he drove the twenty-minute route back to the hotel.

*   *   *

Willa always traveled light. Years of chasing after stories and legends around the world trained her to pack efficiently. Cotton clothing, easily de-wrinkled and well-suited for mixing and matching, shared one suitcase with her personal grooming items. A

28

small satchel held snacks, notebooks, and reading material. Her purse served as her identification container, bank, and junk drawer.

On the morning Lock was preparing his helicopter for his ride into the Amazon, Willa added the unbound document containing Asitr's stories to her luggage. A cumbersome bag with the cut tops of a dozen pineapples made her feel unbalanced as she made her way to the desk. After checking out, she sat in the lobby and waited for Lock.

When Lock arrived, she stood up and embraced him. "I'm all in, one-hundred percent," she said. "Can I join you?"

7

A NEW EDEN

O N THE SECOND MORNING OF CAMPING near the hole that used to be a spring, Lock and Willa awoke to a colorful pile of feathers next to the campfire. There were no fruits or berries, just birds. Familiar rhythmic lyrics made both of them sit up in their sleeping bag and turn their head to the direction of the song.

"We have company," Lock said.

"Duke Duke Duke Duke of Earl, Duke Duke Duke of Earl, Duke Duke Duke of Earl, Duke Duke ..."

The chant continued to grow louder, closer, and soon the sound of bare feet stomping in unison to the rhythm inspired smiles and bobbing heads as the Weareus tribe emerged from the channels in stone where the water from the spring once emptied.

The singers, elbows out, legs bowed, faces set serious, stomped like miniature sumo wrestlers in a circle around the couple. Small naked bodies, with heads ringed in colorful feathers, bobbed left and right in unison with each step they took. The chant grew louder and louder, then suddenly dropped to a hush as another singer, with a crown of blackberry vines, a wooden staff, and a necklace of bright plumage, stepped forward and attempted to solo the lead melody with out-of-tune *wah*'s and *weeooh*'s. The solo attempt was wordless, and comical, like an out-of-tune trumpet solo, but recognizable.

"They are forbidden to sing the verses," whispered Lock.

Thanks to her briefing on the helicopter ride to the bald knob, and the details revealed before Asitr's ashes were scattered into the hole where the spring had been, Willa knew who was coming. She knew the solo singer with the staff, crown, and necklace was the tribal leader. Sitting up in her sleeping bag, lost in the moment, she bopped in tandem with the dancers to the rhythm of the stomp and giggled. This, she knew, was an anthropologist's dream.

After the second circle around Lock and Willa, the backup singers stomped and sang loudly as they filed back down the drop and into the hole, leaving only the soloist behind, arms folded, staring uncomfortably at Willa with the scowl of a man who didn't like what he saw.

"Keep smiling, maintain eye contact, don't stand, and don't touch him," Lock told Willa. "Something's wrong."

Lock rolled out of his sleeping bag and stood naked in front of the chief. As part of his preparations for Willa, he told her he may struggle with the language. He knew less than one hundred words. Those words had to be used only three at a time. Any word could be repeated in a sentence for emphasis, but a fourth word would end conversation and the speaker would be regarded as a fool. Anyone who broke the rule would be shunned for three days, then judged by the chief. If the offender was tapped by the chief's rod on the left shoulder, he could stay with the tribe. If tapped on the right shoulder, he would be sent into the wilderness. As in all things, the chief's decision was final. If the chief ever reversed his decision, a new chief was chosen.

The scowling man in front of Lock was not the old chief. The old chief was a pleasant man. This guy was not.

After a long stare-down brought no words from the chief, Lock gambled. "We welcome visitor," he said, attempting to establish authority in Eden.

"Asitr has changed." The chief retained his scowl and pointed to Willa.

Lock let the misperception go unchallenged.

When Asitr had his first audience with the old chief, the question-answer dialogue was difficult, even for a skilled linguist like Grampy.

"Who are you?" asked Asitr.

"We are us," replied the old chief.

"You have name?"

"I am me."

"Name of all?" Asitr spread his arms, sweeping them in an attempt to communicate he wanted the name of the tribe.

"We are us."

When Grampy and Lock left the protection of the tribe and moved through other tribal territories, they always referred to this tribe as the Weareus. Due to those memories, Lock decided questions or challenges to misperceptions would not be the best way to start a dialogue with the new chief.

"We bring gifts," he said.

"Give to me."

"Come." Lock pointed to the helicopter and began walking, stopping once to glance behind him to check on Willa. She was putting Lock's seersucker robe on, scrambling to catch up.

After reaching the helicopter, Lock opened the door and reached in for the gifts.

"You give bird?"

"No, bird mine. No, no, no bird."

The chief tugged on the door. "I take feather."

Once again, with emphasis, Lock stopped the tugging on the door and growled, "Bird need feather." He turned his eyes away from the chief and rolled his eyes to Willa. "I bring this," he said, and handed Willa's bag of pineapples to the chief. "This is pineapple." Lock kicked at the dirt and set the pineapple top down on the surface, pantomiming it was intended to be eaten.

When the chief picked the pineapple from the ground and bit into a leaf, Willa stifled a laugh.

Silently, Lock pulled another pineapple from the bag, dragged his finger across the yellow bottom and licked the juice. The chief followed suit, smiled, and touched his nose.

Lock reached in again and presented the bag of seeds, but the chief ended the discussion with an invitation in the form of a command.

"You bring tomorrow," he said.

"Tomorrow we bring," answered Lock. He turned to Willa and winked. When he turned his head, the chief pulled himself into the helicopter and grabbed the guitar, banging it against the seats, then reached for Willa's purse.

Willa stepped to Lock's side and whispered in his ear. "Stop him, John. Take control."

You didn't have to understand words to see petulance take the place of the kid-at-Christmas smile on the chief's face. He hopped out of the helicopter, and once again glowered toward Willa, reaching out with his staff and parting her robe.

"I take this," he said, and pulled the robe sleeve down her arm.

Willa, by look and gesture, told Lock not to interfere, then cooperated in removing the garment.

After placing it on himself, the chief turned without more discussion and walked to the exit in the cliff, the robe dragging the ground as he went.

"It was easier when we had nothing to give them," Lock said.

"They are fascinating," Willa replied, "and unpredictable."

Lock placed the seeds back into the helicopter, then slammed the door violently. "Damn," he said. "He took the keys."

"I'm sure you have another ... Don't you?"

"Yeah, I sewed it into the hem of my robe."

Like the boys in the box, the stranded couple had some brainstorming to do

*   *   *

Lock and Willa missed their date for giving their gift of seeds to the Weareus. Their options for leaving Eden were daunting.

"The chief is going to be offended," said Lock. "I should search for where I buried my weapons and hope they still function."

"No," Willa said, "Let's review our options again. We can fix this."

She walked over to the hole where the spring once flowed from the depths and tossed a stone into the chasm. The echo of the rock bouncing off the walls got quieter with each bounce, until neither of them could hear it. No sound rose to the top to indicate the bottom was found.

"We can rule that out," Lock said. "Next?"

Willa sat down on the edge of the chasm and put her head in her hands. "Maybe we should keep trying the radio in the 'copter?"

"We can't drain the battery." Lock sounded weary of going over the same options. "What's next?"

Willa tossed another stone over the side and looked up to the tall cliffs surrounding them. With the voice of the disheartened, she sighed in resignation. "Scaling the cliff is out of the question. Even if we made it to the top, neither of us is going to test the halo of vines hanging down around the peak."

Lock sat next to Willa and put his arm around her. "Let's forget the impossible and the unwise," he said. "Let's figure out how to do the unsafe."

Willa knew what Lock meant. They kept returning to the option they were calling 'Quetzacatl's Door'.

Inspection of the hole, by flashlight, already suggested difficulties. An immediate drop-off of five feet gradually sloped downward until a stone wall blocked the light. Knowing the wall wasn't the end of the opening suggested another drop of undetermined size.

"The Weareus used it to reach Eden," Lock said. "I know it reaches to the river."

Willa didn't like the option. "When you made it to the river, you were pushed along by gravity and cushioned by water. There's no way of knowing the path can be duplicated in air. You couldn't see. The only feature you know exists is a pinch point that nearly ended your journey. The Weareus are tiny. You were skinny then. You've got a belly, and I have a Ruebenesque butt. Once in, the way back out isn't guaranteed." Willa argued her objections, but knew that dangerous was wiser than impossible, and possible was better than unwise. Before Lock responded, she added her acceptance. "I'm going with you."

When the final plans were made, and the equipment was gathered, Willa agreed to stay behind. Vines were cut, braided into rope, then tied around a boulder at the entrance. Willa wrapped them into a harness around Lock's chest. She put both of their mobile phones into Lock's pants pockets to be used as reserve lighting. Next, she wrapped a hammer and machete into a cotton skirt and tied the package onto Lock's belt loops. Their only flashlight she tied to his wrist.

The process, from braiding to equipping, took five days to complete. But, finally, Lock started his descent. His feet were still in the sunlight. He was searching for a hand grip at the first five-foot drop when a flash of brightness stopped him in his tracks.

At the wall where the light stopped, a mass of bright red, green, and blue poked above the gap in front of the wall.

Lock froze, focusing his beam on the top of a Weareus headdress. A face followed. Dark eyes, a broad nose, and finally, two hands clutching the ledge where the light disappeared. The two eyes blinked in the glare of the flashlight and a timid voice cracked the silence.

"I know you," it said.

"Don't be afraid," Lock answered.

"Was long time." The hands, the eyes and the ring of feathers in the hair stayed motionless, like a *'Kilroy was here'* image, until Lock invited the guest into Eden.

"Please, come," Lock said, as he backed out of the entrance and allowed the sunlight to penetrate through the hole. Whispering to Willa while he began to unravel the knot holding his machete, he said, "We have company. Be on guard."

Crawling into the light, a wrinkled face emerged. A smile from the heart lit its eyes, and the deep wrinkles, pushed together in a smile around an almost toothless face, signaled trust. Lock stopped fidgeting with his knot and held out his hand to help the old one out of the opening.

When the body emerged, sagging breasts identified the visitor as a woman.

"You are Lockjaw," she said. Her smile turning to a look of awe, she stared at Willa and put her hands to her mouth, covering her near toothless gasp. "It is true," she said. "Magic."

Glances of confusion between Lock and Willa disturbed their visitor. "You forget me?"

Lock didn't know what to say, and Willa didn't know what was being said. Gathering thoughts took too long, and rolling tears spilled from the old woman's eyes. Her brow wrinkled and her shoulders slumped. "I never forget. I remember friend. You love me. I love you."

The woman shuddered and held her hands toward Willa, as if pleading for mercy.

Suddenly it was clear to Lock. This was the woman who nursed Asitr back to health. The bond between the two was powerful. When he and Grampy had left the tribe and walked into the wilderness, she begged to go with them.

"Sing more songs," she had pleaded as the two of them left the village. "Show me world."

Genuinely touched by her pleas at the time, Asitr felt heartless but practical when he refused her. He couldn't, in good conscience, expose her to the dangers of the journey. He did delay the departure to comfort her and let her know he may never return.

"You want more," Asitr told her.

"Same as Quetzacatl," she replied.

"You are better," Asitr responded.

After tearful hugs, Asitr pulled away from his nurse and walked toward the path, stopping once to turn to her and say, "See in Heaven."

"See in Heaven," she replied.

"Walking into the bush, Grampy's voice broke when he told Lock, "In all my lives, I've never seen a woman with such a loving spirit."

Now, face to face, Lock knew letting the chief believe Asitr had transformed into a 'dark giant woman' was going to be a problem.

"Willa, don't speak," he said. "Embrace this woman like a long-lost friend. I'll explain later. She thinks you're Asitr."

8

"MR. BECKLEY, I DON'T THINK we are going to finish up tonight. I've been listening since eight o'clock this morning. It's now going on eleven p.m. An hour ago, you promised you were nearly done, but you're only up to 2007. You still have eighteen more years to cover. Let's wrap this up for tonight. I'll see you tomorrow morning.

"Okay, Doc. You still have an hour before your mother goes to bed. I know you need to call her."

"My mother?" Dr. Milton's face worked its way from confusion to humor. "Oh, good one. Really good. I get it. I surrender. Best April Fool's joke ever. Did you make all of it up as you went? No. How long have you been working on this? Abrams is going to hear about wasting my vacation."

"I don't know Abrams. I know you're going to call your mother. It's prophecy."

"Prophecy. About my mother's sleeping habits?"

"I'm not a prophet. It's a message from a messenger."

"Mr. Beckley, I have a tried and true method with my patients. I listen before I interact. You are not a patient, so let me say this. I declare you an insanely good April Fool's joke, but a sane man. I hope you didn't have plans this evening. I can't release you until morning."

"Won't happen. You are going to call your mother before her bedtime. Tomorrow, you'll help someone who needs you. After you play your part in a long chain of events, I'll record the results. I'm recording right now."

"Mr. Beckley, stop. I've busted you. And by the way, I see through your trick with the marble prop. My orderlies use the heart monitor to play their music. Weakest part of the joke was pretending that piece of glass was magic."

"How is that done, Doc? Why is it done? Why is a medical device equipped to play music?"

"Right, you don't know about the cloud act. Nice try."

"But the monitor ..." Otis pointed to the plug under the cart. "It wasn't even plugged in after the water spill."

Dr. Milton didn't give the plug a glance. "Good night, Mr. Beckley. Tomorrow, I'll deal with my trickster friend, Dr. Abrams."

"Okay." Otis shrugged. "See you in the morning, Doc."

9

OFFICE OF DR. HENRY MILTON
APRIL 1, 2025 – 11:10 PM

D R. MILTON SAT BEHIND HIS DESK to gather papers, stopping to read a note left by his secretary: *Call your mother.*

Speaking to himself, the doctor muttered, "Enough, already." Then he reached for the phone to congratulate his boss for the day-wasting joke. The number five was lit up in the *Missed Messages* panel. The first message, short and to the point as always, was from his mother: "Call me."

The second message was from Dr. Abrams. "Thanks for taking my patient; I'll make it up to you. I owe you one briefcase."

A briefcase? Dr. Milton glanced at his briefcase, lying on his desk in front of him, then picked it up to examine it. "You look good to me," he said, talking directly to his case.

The third message was, again, from his mother. "Call me."

The fourth call was from the medical supervisor. "Budget meeting Friday. Don't forget."

The fifth call was another message from his mother. "Call me. I'm selling the car tomorrow."

"No," the doctor said out loud. "Not the car."

He pushed back hard into his chair and tried to sort out the urge to call his mother versus the empirical necessity of testing prophecy. Something in his mind was tickling his brain. He was forgetting something. He leaned forward, tapped his papers on the desk, and unlocked his briefcase. When the lid popped, he recoiled from the too-familiar odor of canned fart spray and slammed the lid shut on the too-familiar plastic turd. Doctor Abrams used the same gag last year, on his office chair.

"Scatological-obsessed deviant," he said aloud.

Milton put his elbows on the desk and pondered the research he had done on false memories and the information the brain uses to trigger the recovery of buried memories. He mentally thumbed through files of theories collected while studying brain function. Long ago, he developed a methodology for dealing with those itchy little snippets of memory hiding in his brain.

Eventually, the associated memories of his father's car, his session with Otis Beckley, and the briefcase joke collided on one of the smaller lanes where synapses lose their sense of direction. After colliding, his lost synapses fired, navigated in unison to a more traveled neural highway, then manifested themselves into conscious memory. When his mental images gelled, and the itching stopped, Dr. Milton reached for the phone and called his mother.

"Hi, mom. About the car."

10

T HE YEAR 2005 WAS A BIG ONE FOR THE MILTON FAMILY. The
future Dr. Henry Milton was following in his father's
footsteps. Like his father, Dr. Simon Milton, Henry was accepted
into medical school at NYU.

Henry wasn't walking an identical path. His father graduated
in 1976 and began a successful practice in proctology. Henry was
going to study psychiatry. He much preferred exploring the
canyons of the mind to spelunking the recesses of the rectum.

As a celebration of his father's 2005 retirement, and a thank
you for the college fund which made NYU possible, Henry made
plans for a car gathering dust in the shed behind the garage.
Intuitively, he knew his idea would be the perfect gift.

His parents spoke reverently about his 1960 Chevy Super
Sport convertible. When Henry was young, the talk was about
converting the car into a hot rod. As the years went on, and Simon
matured, the talk was about a less complicated and time-consuming
restoration.

When his mother, Doris, talked about the car, she centered on memories of the courting years, cruising the weekends away, top down, to the sounds of Dion, The Platters, and Elvis. With her sunglasses on, hair blowing in the wind, and the oldies serenading them on the radio, she knew the two of them were cool. While musing about those years, her voice grew soft, and her eyes focused somewhere in the past. After his mother's reveries, his father always added, "I had more bugs in my teeth than the Hell's Angels."

Talk of restoring the car was happy talk and nothing more. Dr. Simon Milton never had the time to begin his project.

On a warm late-spring evening in 2005, Dr. Simon and his wife Doris were at the computer, happily engaged in planning to see the world through the eyes of foot-loose retirees, freed from the shackles of schedules and responsibilities. Standing at the front door, ready to deliver the perfect gift of thanks and love, their son Henry began pounding loudly, shouting, "Hurry! The garage! Hurry!"

Startled by the urgent knock, Simon and Doris stiffened. Recognizing the voice made them jump to their feet and run after their son, yelling, "What is it? What is it?"

After flipping the light switch in the garage, they gasped. In front of the retirees was parked a fully restored 1960 Chevy Super Sport convertible. The sudden silence, the twin gasps, the wide eyes were better than words. Henry's gift was a happy shocker.

The mother and father circled the car while dad asked questions. "Is it all original? What did you replace? Did you do this yourself?"

The answers were given as Henry leaned over the driver's seat and turned the key.

"Listen to this motor purr," he said. "All the work was professionally done. The seats, the tires, and the top are new. The dents, the rust, and the scratches are gone. It's been undercoated. The hardest thing was finding a replacement for the faded bumper sticker. Really, dad, *Elect McGovern-Eagleton* was hard to find when it was current."

"Look at that," Doris said, "I feel like jumping in and taking off now. Maps be damned." Sliding into the passenger seat, she reached for the radio. "Look, Simon, the radio is still set on our station."

When the old AM radio blared, they heard the words:

They can't do that babe, stay calm. Bill needs us ... Po? ... Po!

Stop.

The frantic plea was followed by the static noise of dead air.

"Turn it off," the senior Milton shouted above the noise. Who needs a radio?"

To everyone's surprise, the old doctor started shuffling around the car singing in his gruff tone-deaf voice.

Yeah, I'm the kinda guy who likes to run around.
Never in one place,
I move from town to town.

"You better not finish that next verse," Doris shouted in mock anger. She jumped out of her seat and stuck out her arm in the hitchhiker's pose. When Simon held his hand out toward her, she danced the stroll over to him and they locked hands, the two of them, dancing and singing like stiff bobbysoxers.

We're the wanderers,
Yeah, the wanderers,

The two dancers raised one clasped hand above their heads and Doris twirled. Raising his free hand above his head, Simon pointed his fingers skyward and shook them in the boogy-hands move.

We roam from town to town,
Living life without a care,
Happy as a clown ...

The future Dr. Milton clapped in rhythm, laughing at his first real peek into his parents' past. In multi-generational parlance, he shouted encouragement. "Party on kids. Boogy oogy oogy."

The dancing couple leaned away from each other, jazz-handing joyfully. In that moment, their grip loosened. Doris stumbled into the garage wall, and the dancing Simon clutched his chest, then fell backwards, dead before he hit the ground.

Conjuring buried memories from the past overcame Dr. Milton's disdain, but not his skepticism. He prided himself in his ability to rethink entrenched beliefs, when challenged, so he weighed the value of empirical testing against intuitive recognition. It made sense his mother would want to remove a visual reminder of the tragic night. He reached for the phone.

"I don't want to disappoint you, son," she said. "I'm going through reverse nesting. I'm old and need to sweep out the cobwebs before I move on."

Glancing at the clock on his office wall, after hanging up the phone, the doctor noticed it wasn't quite midnight and wondered who it was he might be helping tomorrow. He was beginning to accept the idea of prophecy. Still, realizing how easily false memories were planted in Harvard's *Manchurian Candidate* project, he knew empirical corroboration would be a good idea.

Before he went to bed, Henry figured out some tests to run before he tossed his skepticism away altogether.

11

"OKAY, MR. BECKLEY, I'M LISTENING. Where were we?"
"Good morning, Doc. Welcome to the link-in-the-chain club. What test do you have for me before we continue?"

"What makes you think I have tests for you?"

"You have a scientific, but open mind. What's the test?

"Is your marble recording?"

"Yes."

"If I removed it from the room, would it continue to record?"

"Yes."

"Then, with your permission?"

"Be my guest, Doc."

*   *   *

After ten minutes with the marble, Dr. Milton returned to the room and walked past his chair to the monitoring equipment. He glanced at Otis, gave him a wink, then bent over, confirming the monitor equipment was still unplugged.

"Sorry I took so long, Mr. Beckley, I don't know if it recorded. I couldn't figure out how to play it back. Would you assist?"

"I'll need to do that. It's attuned to me. Ready, Doc?"

"Go ahead." Dr. Milton's voice filled the room.

Page three, April the second, two thousand twenty-five. Lawrence Register. All the news that fits onto twenty pages of ads ... Just my little joke, Mr. Beckley ... From page three.

More attacks in Nineveh ... Drone attacks killed twelve civilians and three Israeli troops in the city of Nineveh on Monday ... Ms. Hoopla returns to California, tells fans she has kicked her shyness problems but struggles now with sex addiction ...

Hmm ... I see there is a sale on 'Tooth White' at Government Surplus Emporium, this week only. That's the news of the day, Mr. Beckley, but I have one more test ... walking down the hallway, looking for ... Here we go. Mr. Douglas, hold up. Are you listening to the radio?'

Yessir.

Which station?

KPOX, sir.

What is playing right now?

Uh ... Gorgonzola Eats the Po-Po.

Thank you. Do you have the time?

To do what?

The time of day.

Oh, uh, yes. It's 9:04.

Thank you, Jarvis. You've been helpful.

"Boy Howdy, Doc. What kind of music is that? Stinky cheese, eating the police. I don't get it."

"Gorgonzola is a cartoon character. He teaches recycling to children. The song is a tongue-in-cheek, post-hop tune about the ecological value of eating the permanently poor."

"Wow. I have a lot of catching up to do. Was your test successful?"

"I'll think on it. Let's get back to your story. This old woman, is she part of your chain?"

"An important link."

"Don't think of me as your doctor. I don't have a protocol for you. At this point I just want to know how this turns out."

"Me too, doc. I'll tell you what I know."

"Fine. Do you know how this woman becomes important?"

12

THE ROSETTA STONE OF *QUIPU*

A SITR'S OLD NURSE WAS A SPINDLY FIGURE. A small person, even by Weareus standards. By Savant standards, she would have been slight of build, but not short. As a descendant of Quetzacatl, much of her genetic makeup came from the Savant.

When Quetzacatl's genes were introduced into her tribe, they established an odd pattern. They popped up every third generation, in only one child. This chain led to a history of grandparent to grandchild sessions, passing down Asitr's stories and talking in illegal sentences while sitting by the river. The storytelling always took place across from the hole where the water flowed from Eden. The secret ritual was called the rite of speaking in tongues.

For the nameless nurse, there would be no ritual to pass down. In spite of *knowing* all the males in the tribe, as has always been the custom, she was barren.

Just as Asitr knew his lives of storytelling were at an end, she knew there was nobody in her tribe who could take part in the tradition. Her anguish at being the last in the chain was a source of inward pressure, relieved only by thoughts of leaving her tribe to see the world.

When Lock and Willa landed in Eden, she was eager and ready for change but thought it might be more prudent to hide her Savant skills until she understood more English. Her English skills were good enough to know the dark, giant, woman wasn't Asitr.

When Lock told Willa, "Treat her like a long-lost friend. I'll explain later. She thinks you're Asitr," the nurse decided listening was more prudent than talk. Instead of engaging in a gabfest, the old woman put a lid on the pressure to speak freely and delivered the chief's message.

"You not welcome. Stay away."

The news was a big problem for Lock and Willa. They needed to find a way to get one of the helicopter keys. Worse, if they couldn't get to the river, they had no access to water. Lock predicted they had a six-week supply, if they didn't bathe.

Willa's reaction to their predicament was understandable. "Separate sleeping bags, please."

As the day wore on, the old nurse stayed near the worried couple, playing with unfamiliar items, trying to be helpful with meal preparations, and always listening.

That night, around their campfire, decisions were made. The old nurse spent the night soaking in the serious talk, absorbing new understanding of the English language. In the process, she discovered why Lock allowed the chief to believe in Asitr's transformation. She forgave him, but still she decided to play a role of her own design.

For the present, she would be the go-between in the negotiations Lock and Willa were planning. To be successful, she needed to be a Weareus. There would be a better time for her to quit her tribe and leave Eden with Lock and Willa. Like a character in a fictional tale told to her by Asitr, she decided to be like a girl named Dorothy, help her friends, then escape into the sky, flying over the rainbow and into the world.

Before the sun rose, Lock took the flashlight and walked cautiously up the hill to the bald knob at Eden's peak. Memories of Dave's encounter with the Laberria serpent slowed his ascent.

Slowing down even more to look for landmarks near where he buried his weapons, Lock despaired. All his landmarks were long-gone trees and berry patches.

Before Lock reached the peak, he saw the glint of the moon reflecting off the helicopter window. His first visit to Eden began with watching a helicopter cross the moon on its way back home. Tonight, he watched the moon cross in the glare of his helicopter window and felt time was folding into itself. Everything was repeating, only warped, backwards, and threatening.

If he knew what was to take place on the moon in eighteen years, he might have laughed. On this night, he was melancholy. For that reason, after removing the seeds from the 'copter, he sat facing east in the cockpit, tuned his guitar, then waited.

When the first sliver of light appeared over the cliffs, Lock began softly finger picking an old tune, handed down from Pagan Gaelic tribes, converted into a Christian hymn, then made popular in modern times by a Muslim singer, for the purpose of praise for a new day. When Lock began singing the words, "*Morning has broken,*" the echo inside the cockpit increased his feeling of solitude. For the first time since he lost Grampy, the solitude felt right.

Lock let his last note hang in the air while tears of self-pity gave way to tears of renewal.

In the bushes, the old nurse reacted to the sound of the guitar and the words of the song with her own tears of joy. Then she backed away to make it down the hill before she could be caught in the light.

Lock lingered before he returned to the campsite. When he came back down the hill, Willa was awake, preparing breakfast. The old nurse sat on a rock, listening to Ray Charles on Willa's CD player.

"I have seeds." Lock held the bag over his head while he shouted at the mesmerized nurse. "Make chief happy."

"She can't hear you," Willa said, "Let her listen. We have pancakes for breakfast. Bugs got into the mix, so I strained them out, we should eat them before they're totally ruined."

"Pancakes take a lot of water. Go slow." Lock was suddenly hungry after catching a whiff, but he couldn't help but recalculate the water supply.

"The old gal is going to bring water back after she talks to the chief," Willa said. "I think we'll have peace by this evening. Who could resist our trade offer?"

Lock set his seeds down next to the other offerings. Their opening offer would be seeds, a cell phone with a magically glowing light, a spray bottle of perfume, and a belt with a pattern of stars tooled into the leather.

After breakfast, Willa changed the batteries in the CD player while the old nurse watched. "Make music play," she said to her attentive audience. "You very curious."

Lock wrapped the bundle of trade items together, securing them with the belt, and tied the package and a canteen to the end of their hand-braided rope. "For water," he said, tapping his finger on the canteen.

"For water," replied the nurse. "Now, I go."

When the old woman went down the hole to the river, Lock and Willa fed out the slack. The slow, steady progress ended, followed by three tugs on the rope to let them know she was at the river. The old woman's progress was made without a hitch.

The two adventurous lovers stayed nervously at the entrance above, waiting for another three tugs to announce the old nurse was returning.

"Ya know, John, we really have to come up with a name for her. If it's not against tribal law."

While Willa allowed herself to worry over the old woman's safety, she began feeling guilty. It didn't feel right to think of her as a nameless tribal member.

"How 'bout Florence Nightingale," Lock answered. "Maybe Clara Barton?"

"Too defining," Willa countered. "She's Wonder Woman."

Hours passed before the rope tugged. Willa marked the rope with lipstick so the distance to the river could be measured, then pulled the slack in as the old nurse made her ascent. From the look on her face as she crawled back into the light, they knew the news wasn't good.

"Chief want bird. Want bird tomorrow."

Serious, sometimes contentious, debate swirled between Lock and Willa. Ideas were floated; ideas were shot down.

Lock wanted to go down the hole and hammer the opening wider, so he could fit through. "I'll kick that little tyrant's ass and bring the key back," he said.

The old nurse stomped her foot and spoke the idea down. "Not outrun poison."

"Poison?" Willa asked. "What kind? Poison darts?"

Willa's choice of plans was in more negotiations. "I want to be on friendly terms with this tribe, John. Let's offer to get the robe in return for a promise to come back with bigger magic. Tell them we want to join the tribe when we return. I do want to study them and their relationship to Quetzacatl."

With a loud sigh, the nurse walked over to Willa, stood on her tip toes, squinted, staring directly into Willa's face. Her face lines looked more like the wrinkled snarl of an angry dog than the familiar maps of wisdom. Her soft, wet eyes disappeared under gray brows.

After an uncomfortably long silence, she asked, in English, "Want join tribe?"

"Yes," Willa answered.

"Ready for ritual?"

"I don't know. What is ritual?"

"All men boom boom."

"Boom boom?"

The nurse bent at the knees, placed her fists in front of her pelvis, and thrust her hips back and forth, repeating the word — *boom, boom, boom, boom* — over and over again, while rolling her eyes at Lock.

"Last all day. Last all night. Then they vote. Then chief decide. Chief like Foop. Stupid and selfish. Might say no. Might say yes. You want try?"

The response from Willa was quick, "No, hell no."

Lock stumbled a little. "Absolutely out of ... wait," he said. "You know about Foop? Yes, of course, I mean no. Yes to Foop; no to ritual." Lost in the two thoughts, he completely mangled the attempt to keep his word count to three. "Oh, yes, I see. Asitr told you his mother's story ... In three-word sentences?"

"I can help. Speak like world?" she asked.

A confused silence met her question, so she asked again, adding details. "Speak like world? Want leave tribe. Want see world. Want own name. Need permission."

"Permission?" Lock suddenly understood, but wanted to verify what the old woman was asking, "Yes, speak freely. Leave with us? What your name?"

Willa grabbed onto Lock's arm when she realized what was happening. "Yes, speak. Must have name."

"Call me Dorothy." Dorothy didn't waste her time. She jumped right into speaking freely. "I have questions to ask you. Is the feather you want silver like flashlight? Is it hard like flashlight, flat, with round head and teeth on skinny neck? Is it what you call a key?" The newly named Dorothy pulled the key from her head band, holding it out for inspection. "Chief wears one around his neck. When he walks on his robe, he tears it When this fell out, I picked it up."

Morning had broken again, in the middle of the day.

13

BENDING BRAINS IN A BOX

T HE ONE-HUNDRED PERCENT CLUB WAS STUCK. After a week of
mostly silent thinking, the list of things they knew for certain
remained at their original three items. I suggested breaking up the
club and starting a new one.

Robert took the suggestion as a surrender. "I'm going to find
a way out," he said. "With you or without you."

"I think we're limiting ourselves into failure," I countered.

Asitr agreed we should try to explore the speculative.

For the next few days, Robert tended to focus his energy on
his own anger. Kae'Lairy was his target.

I suggested mining for clues in Kae'Lairy's motivations. "We
should pool our process and revisit one theory at a time," I
proposed. "I suggest sticking with brainstorming Kae'Lairy's
motivation."

"I like it," Asitr said. "I'm stuck on dumb. Where should we
start?"

"Something basic. I keep wondering if his intentions are something as simple as just being old-fashioned evil. Do you believe he's fallen?"

Robert asked Asitr's opinion and gave his own. "What do you think, Asitr? Who is the baddest guy? I believe Kae'Lairy's cruel, but God is cruel to let him keep us."

Asitr didn't want to get caught in the middle of an apples-and-oranges discussion. I didn't either. I wanted to go into diagnostic mode. Robert was putting up a false either-or detour. Asitr knew debating two abstract conclusions, prior to discussing facts and definitions, would lead to entrenchment in a rut of defending egos. Any third option, very often the better option, was left unconsidered. He didn't know if discussing Kae'Lairy's motives would get them anywhere, but it was a beginning, not a rut.

"Robert," he began, "help us out. I have faith everything is going to turn out okay. Let's brainstorm on any and all reasons Kae'Lairy might have for what he is doing, then follow up."

At first it looked like Robert was going to be obstinate. "What makes you an expert, Asitr? You always think you're doing the right thing, but it … never turns out … well." Robert's voice tailed off.

I think he realized, mid-sentence, he also was prone to the curse of good intentions with bad results. So, why not Kae'Lairy, too?

Asitr drove his point home with another question. "When you ran after the Kotex to save your mom, were you a bad guy, or just mistaking the situation?"

"I did the wrong thing. I was only little."

I was happy Robert didn't run away and hide in his fortress of silence. I rewarded him by putting the ball in his court. "Where should we start, Robert? Have any ideas?"

"Yes, Kae'Lairy could be a good or bad angel. God could be trapped, like us, but trapped in a cage he made himself. God won't lie, so he is vulnerable to those he's made promises to."

"It's possible," I mumbled. "In some universe."

"Maybe we are on the sharp edge of free will, Robert," Asitr added. "God can't help us escape, and Kae'Lairy is an angel running after Kotex."

I brought the discussion back around to figuring out Kae'Lairy's motivations. "Let's keep that idea in mind. The three-way-trap idea is interesting," I said. "Right now, let's say we brainstorm on Kae'Lairy being well intentioned, but wrong. What is he wrong about? He's afraid of us being on the loose? Why?"

"Is there anyone on earth who speaks the old tongue?" Asitr grabbed for the only item on the one-hundred percent list that stood out. "Robert, does Po know the language?"

"No, I'm sure she doesn't. All the Savant are dead, right?"

A moment of thought passed, then Asitr and I spoke at once. In the Doppler effect of dueling voices, neither answer was clear, so Asitr gave me the floor. "Go ahead," he said. "What were you saying?"

"I said we were forgetting somebody — a whole lot of somebodies. Alayat also knows the old tongue. I don't know how many other angels do, but I'd bet anything the number is large. We're the only humans who know the language."

"Oh!" Robert blurted out the word loudly, as if he was just smacked in the face by a two-by-four. "Bill's friend, Stan. I've heard the two of them speaking the language. I forgot about Stan."

"You can feel free to forget about Stan," Asitr said. "If you're referring to Stanley Goodhope, he's dead and gone, and the world is better off for it. Let's leave him out of this discussion."

"Okay, Asitr." I jumped back in quickly to make sure Robert didn't ask more questions about Alazam's host. "We have a set of beings who speak the language. If we eliminate all angels and all the dead, we have a subset of three humans who speak the language. All three are in this box."

Robert corrected my oversight. "Sorry, Otis. I think you're forgetting Asitr is in the subset of dead humans."

A pause followed Robert's observation. The term 'pregnant pause' was entirely appropriate. New ideas and new sets of questions were born in the silence.

Asitr suggested some things to discuss. "Kae'Lairy is being shunned for a reason. Is it because you guys are missing from your appointed time in the short life? Or because he hasn't delivered Alayat to his judgment? Should he be taking me home to Heaven?"

Robert couldn't help but revisit his doubts. "You're assuming Heaven is your home. You're assuming there is a Heaven. If we walk down that road of investigation, we have to assume your faith is a valid reality. We have to assume those promises you talk about are actually from God and not wishful thinking. That's a lot of assumptions."

"If you want irrefutable proof, before we investigate, you're missing the point of the short life. If you want to rule out the possibility of an interactive creator, you're leaving a lot of evidence uninvestigated. Don't be that guy. Look for designs and you'll catch a glimpse of him. Once you recognize he is there, don't think you know him, and don't interfere with other people's search for him. God will recognize the sincere, no matter what their conclusions are. I know I'm drifting off into being preachy, but if we're going to refuse to look down a road because there are unprovable observations in the path, then we should go back to the one-hundred percent club. Is that what you want Robert?"

"No, Asitr. I'll walk your path with you, but I want to point out the poison ivy in the blueberry bushes, if I see it."

"Good answer, Robert."

"Great," I added quickly. I was encouraged by the cooperative direction. "So we are agreed. We are going to begin discussing theory based on the observation that a well-intentioned angel is shunned because he's troubled by two souls and one spirit who speak a dead language. The souls are kept from living their time on earth, and the spirit is denied access to Heaven. Why?"

"Don't forget Alayat," Asitr said. "He's also denied access to Heaven for his judgment. Am I forgetting anything?"

"Yes," Robert said, "You can't forget what we don't know yet. Where should we start?"

"I'd like to suggest a computer concept," I began. "If I understand things correctly: angels are what they are. They are designed with attributes to carry out specific tasks or functions. A computer is similar. They can't go beyond their firewalls. They can't calculate beyond their maximum. Each one is different. If you could bar-code their abilities, they would show much different sets of bars in almost every category. The one area they all share in common is in the concept of nothing. Every computer will have a nervous breakdown if confronted with pondering the concept of nothing. I'm suggesting Kae'Lairy is unable to function appropriately, because he is stuck on a decision he sees as a nothing. Possibly, he's forbidden by his firewalls to choose a corrective action. Maybe he's too limited to imagine a resolution."

"You're suggesting he's confronted with indecision, because he can't find a corrective action in his programming? Leading to an option he can't see? A "nothing" option? Is that what you're suggesting?" Asitr sounded excited. He saw how easily my theory fit into Enoch's description of angels as limited, while humans were designed to become "more", with unconditional free will.

Robert didn't have my talent for numbers, or Asitr's experience with Enoch, but he was super-smart and highly motivated to get back home to see his child. His intuitive nature was alive in our investigation. "What did Kae'Lairy say to you, Otis? Before he put you in the box?"

The answers Asitr and I gave took us another step down the path we were exploring.

"He told me I was justified in dissipating Alazam," I said. Then, I remembered his introduction. "He told me he was a mighty bondsman, messenger of the Lord, and protector of the throne. He sounded pretty puffed up about his resume.

"Protector of the throne?" Asitr repeated the words. "He gave me the same spiel. What is the protector of the throne?"

"What is the throne of God anyway? Are we a threat to the throne?"

Bobby had just asked yet another question worth pondering.

14

INTO THE WORLD

L OCK HAD A HISTORY OF BEING IN SITUATIONS where good outcomes never came easy. When Dorothy produced the helicopter key, and began speaking in excellent English, his mind went straight to looking for the big ugly surprise.

It was Willa who jumped into the moment and seized it. The woman, who spent a good part of her career interviewing *modernized* tribes kept in tribal preserves and dreamed of studying uncivilized people in their natural environment, didn't waste a moment to abandon her dream.

"What are we waiting for?" she asked. "Forget all the camping gear. Let's hop on the bird and fly."

Dorothy sprinted ahead of them, excited. In the moment, she reverted to her tribal language, whooping in a tone full of awe, "I see world!"

The helicopter started with a cough and sputter. Lock continued to expect something to go wrong and Willa scanned the rocks for naked, horny, little men, waiting to grab her and welcome her into the tribe. Dorothy climbed on top of the golden bull in the back and pressed her face to the window. "Up, up," she said. "Over the rainbow."

Not another word came from Dorothy until, after skimming the sea of green, the helicopter flew past a river village. It was the buildings that got Dorothy excited. They were the largest structures she had ever seen.

"Is New York?" she asked.

Reverting to her tribal speech made Dorothy seem child-like. Willa was both charmed by her and scared for her. Her stomach squirmed, and she paused before answering the question. "No, no," she started, "New York is …" A pang choked Willa in mid-sentence. "New York is bigger."

"Up bigger? To throw paper from high-up on Buffalo Child Long-Lance?"

"Yes, but in every way, much bigger. Too big for us."

"Oh, I see. Too big for me. Many people might not like me. I would try hard. I would smile and show both my teeth. They will see I can be often friendly."

"Everyone will love you, Dorothy." Willa spotted another village and pointed. "Look at this one."

Dorothy pressed her face to the window again, remaining wordless beyond the occasional, sudden "*ooh*" as each village they passed grew bigger than the last.

When they approached a village with a double rainbow arching over its center, she broke her silence, screaming suddenly like a teenage girl. "Over the rainbow! We fly over the rainbow!"

Lock turned and flew straight at the twin arches, but he let Dorothy know the rainbow was like the Savant. "It will hide when we get close. Watch it start to melt away. Before we can fly over it, we will scare it off."

"Then fly away. Let the rainbow alone, to stay pretty."

Willa leaned into Lock. "Dorothy's a rainbow, John. We can't take her to the airport. They'll separate us."

"We have another option, babe. We're going to Sam's island."

"Pineapple Sam? He has an island?"

"He owns it. His wife's tribe lives on it."

"You've known him awhile? You can trust him?"

"He flew the big helicopter at the Grand Canyon when we captured the Shem."

Willa relaxed as miles and miles of green floated by. She was grateful for time to think about how to fit Dorothy into the world, but couldn't ignore time was running out to come up with a plan. The villages were crowding closer together as they flew nearer to civilization.

Lock passed over villages big enough to be called towns. Next, bright lights ahead hinted of the first large mainland city. It was the landmark he was looking for. He veered toward the Panama islands zone, leaving the glow of Panama City at twilight on his left, a sunset behind him, and dark clouds straight ahead.

Dorothy had seen many a wonderful sunset. She saw seasonal storms up close and personal. She had never seen a glow over the land like the lights of civilization.

"How big is their campfire?" she asked.

Willa focused on the cloud ahead of them. The sky turned suddenly, deeply, darker.

Behind them, a fierce red sun sprayed orchid and mango splashes onto the blue-sky palette. Normally, the display would have been the star of the show. On this evening, it wasn't even a distraction.

"We're heading into a storm," Lock called out. "I need to fly under the clouds." With one eye on the gas gauge, he decided not to circle and wait out the storm. He checked his GPS and relaxed. "Less than four miles," he called out. "We're going in."

Willa sat back in her seat, recoiling from a cloud in front of them. "It looks alive," she said. "Scary."

Dorothy didn't seem to notice the oncoming storm. She was losing her adrenaline and starting to let worries close in.

Why do people need to make such big fires? Why is New York too big for me? Does God want me to stay where he put me? Why did I come? Why am I here? Who will like me and give me a home?

Nervously, she began to rub the etchings on the head of the golden calf, realizing her adventure wasn't going to be all berries and fish. Tracing the odd lines with her finger, she thought she noticed a pattern and looked closer.

A sudden flash of light, so white it burned the eyes, turned the sunset to pastel and everything else to black and white. Lightning surrounded the helicopter and crackled, leaving behind the smell of burning hair. The dome light went dark.

Dorothy squeezed her eyes tight, still scratching nervously at the idol's etched head. She opened them briefly when Lock told her it was going to be okay.

"I see the island up ahead."

A stubborn, lingering flash of light from a far-off burst illuminated the inside of the cabin, and Dorothy saw the etchings she had been tracing. "Is something," she called out, then she screamed when the startling boom of the distant lightning rattled the helicopter.

"Yep, this is really something," Lock shouted above a loud push of wind and the sudden slapping of rolling rain curtains diving into the windshield.

"The shiny beast, it is something." Dorothy shrieked at another burst of lightning surrounding the helicopter and dove over the seat into Willa's lap, no longer caring about etchings on a golden cow. "God doesn't want me to fly!" she shouted.

"It's only lightning!" Willa screamed the words without realizing it. Her attempt to comfort Dorothy came across as a cry for help.

The helicopter swayed in the wind gusts from nose to tail rotor, making several sudden, short drops and recoveries. Finally, the view through the pilot's windshield showed a narrow sandy spot of beach with jumping waves and bending palms. Through the rhythmic bands of window-slapping sheets of water, the beach looked like it was darting back and forth, closing too fast, then, *whoomp.*

The helicopter came down hard. The ground was soft, but uneven. A sudden tilt brought a blade into contact with a bending palm, and the helicopter whipped a half turn, then suddenly stopped. The inertia pulled Lock and Willa sideways in their seat belts. A flash of gold caromed off the back of Willa's seat and the idol burst heavily through the passenger door of the copter. A screaming Dorothy followed.

Big fists of raindrops, pushed into the cockpit by wind, belted Lock and Willa in their face while they attempted to reorient themselves to the tilted, motionless helicopter. Willa covered her eyes and looked through the slats of her fingers. In a flash of lightning, she caught a snapshot of Dorothy flailing in a low cluster of palmettos.

Lock opened his door and it flew out of his grip, blown by the wind howling through the missing passenger door. When he tried to climb out, he couldn't lift himself off his seat. He thought he must have been paralyzed, until his shock cleared, and he realized he was still wearing his seat belt. When he unlatched his belt, he slid toward Willa. "Hang on to something," he yelled, "I'm going to undo your seat belt."

"Dorothy's stuck in the — *Ow!*" Willa screamed when she braced herself with her foot, and a sharp pain stabbed her ankle. Her pain cry echoed extra loudly, because the wind stopped suddenly. The howling was gone. So too, were the big lights on the helicopter. Two blinks and they went dead. Only the red flashers kept working.

The rain continued to fall, but down, not hard and sideways. Chill crept into their bodies, and worry for Dorothy filled the places where fear had been. Before they could even call her name, she ran up to them, hair full of orange sand, body scraped by palmetto leaves, and a trickle of blood running with the rain from her nose and dripping off her chin. She had a message for them.

"Mushka! Thank you, that was new for me." She walked in circles, voice excited, arms flapping. She was rambling in shock. "Would I fly one more time? I will wait first. No! Not wait. I will not fly starting now." She pounded her tiny fist into her palm for emphasis. "I will never fly again. *Hooga mushka!* God has put me right here in the rain, and right here in the rain I will live. I am home. I choose to see only the world I can see with my feet on the ground." She ended her declaration by clasping her hands under her chin, rolling her shoulders forward, bowing her head, and shivering from her knees to her lips.

Willa, hopping on her good leg, retrieved her laptop from the floor of the helicopter, then pulled her suitcase to the ground and sat down, opening it in the rain. "You need to put something on," she said.

Dorothy chose the white cotton skirt Willa wore on the beach the night Lock had approached her. She tried wearing the skirt over her head like a cowl, then draped loosely off her neck, and finally over her shoulder and wrapped around her waist. After she pronounced herself satisfied, Willa told her she looked like Mahatma Gandhi.

"Is she pretty?" asked Dorothy.

Willa was saved from answering by the approaching glow of flashlights.

Lock stiffened his body and spoke in a loud whisper. "Where is the idol?"

"In the scratching bushes," answered Dorothy, pointing toward the palmettos.

"Don't tell anyone," Lock said. Then, he called to the men with flashlights, "Over here! Help! We're over here!"

Two men emerged from the vegetation and shined flashlights on the trio. Their greeting was terse, but welcome. "Follow us to the village. We'll have lights soon."

The trio followed the dim light, Lock, acting as a crutch for Willa, who hopped down the dark path on one foot. Dorothy, shivering, disheveled, brushing sand from her hair, wiping blood from her face, and tripping over wet Gandhi diapers, skipped merrily, as if she was heading down the Yellow Brick Road.

15

THE MORE YOU KNOW, THE MORE YOU WARP

I N THE BOX, FAR FROM THE FRENZY ON EARTH, brainstorming began as a healthy distraction. After days of animated argument and collaboration, each of us formed our own pet theory. Well, not so organized as a theory. We had differing gut feelings.

I thought it likely we were overlooking a clue in Kae'Lairy's behavior. It was out of character for him to give us a gift. Why did he give us the Asteroid game? How did he know there was a pile of video games in the debris field? How did they get there? Why were they there?

Robert responded to my curiosity with sarcasm. "Oh, now I get it," he said. "Kae'Lairy was studying the games to figure out how to make a return-to-previous-save option. He could use a do-over button."

Asitr's pet theme was the protecting-the-throne mystery. "I can't visualize a scenario where we could be a threat. I can't rule it out. I can't think about anything else," he said.

Robert didn't want to debate. He wanted us to accept his premise that God had promised himself into a corner, and we were innocent men with grievances.

"That's an abstract conclusion," I let my frustration with Robert spill out in a formal argument, "completely fabricated by an imaginative interpretation of scripture and accepted without knowing the foundational context to support it."

"Agreed," Robert replied. "I got nothin' else."

"On the other hand," I said. "Why video games in space?"

"Let's stay quiet for a while and think," said Asitr. "Give it some time. Like Robert says, we've got nothing."

Ya' know, it never fails. When given quiet, hard-thinkin', focus-driven time to solve one problem, something else pops out of the mind. I was the first to get off track and break the silence. A question kept intruding in my thoughts, and I finally had to ask.

"Hey Robert, I have to know. Why did you want to give the *Asteroid* computer sound capabilities?"

"Oh, I want to make a Christmas album."

"Really? Like singing Christmas songs?"

"Yeah. Leave me alone, I'm trying to think."

After another quiet period of thinking, it was Robert who again went off-topic. "If I went back to earth today, would I be younger than my child? How does that work? The space-time continuum thingy?"

"It's theory," I said, "backed up with mathematical equations, proving the possibility that space, in the three dimensions, renders time a relative concept."

"Relative to what?" Robert asked.

"Relative to spatial viewpoint. You know, how old is that light beam in my eye kind of thing."

"It's a logic problem disguised as a mathematical equation," Asitr interjected. "An exercise in measurements and definitions, with no application for the real world."

"The real world?" I asked. I'm a numbers guy. I love the order in the numbers. There is no 'real' world without the design and there's no design without numbers. No application? How could Asitr disbelieve numbers? I thought a defense of digits was in order.

"You can make mysteries definable with numbers," I told them. "You can manipulate matter. Nano engineers have commanded numbers to arrange quarks into a microscopic ten-micron guitar with tunable strings. You can use numbers to slam basic elements into each other at such high speed they transform into more complex elements. You can numerically manipulate vibrations to make music, form words, burn metals, or force the brain to malfunction. We, ourselves, manufactured a gizmo by the numbers and dissipated an evil spirit. That's for starters. Numbers rule. Logic is individualized and intuitive. Get two people together, and logic becomes relative to inexact definitions of words. Get two mathematicians together, and numbers provide a platform for stability in reasoning."

I thought I'd killed it, crushed his logic-worship with, well, logic.

"Do you have an equation to solve our problem?" Asitr asked with uncustomary sarcasm.

"No."

Robert sounded annoyed with us. "If you don't understand the time warping thing, just say so. What's a logic problem disguised as a math equation anyway?"

"There is no such thing as warping time," Asitr replied. "It's illogical. Everything in space is moving at different rates, but the march of time goes on, stable and eternal."

"You didn't answer his question," I said.

"I can give you an example. You may have already heard it. Three salesmen at a convention. They're at a hotel with only one room available. It's the last vacant room in town. Have you heard it?"

Our silence told Asitr to go on with his example.

"Okay. Three salesmen and one room. The three of them agree to share the room, so they ask the desk clerk how much money each of them needed. The room rate was twenty-five dollars. The clerk tried to divide the twenty-five dollars by three, but he wasn't very good at fractions, so he took the easy way out. "That's ten dollars each," he told them.

"After the three men went up to the room, the clerk struggled with his conscience. Before the shift change, he decided he would go to the room and return the extra five dollars. In the elevator, he tried to figure out how much each man should get back. Predictably, he was unable to pull his numbers together, so he took the easy way out again. He put two dollars in his pocket and gave each of the salesmen a one-dollar refund.

"Now, the three men have each paid nine dollars apiece for the room. That's twenty-seven dollars. The clerk has two dollars in his pocket, for a total of twenty-nine dollars. Where did the other dollar go?"

I'd heard the riddle before, but I knew if Robert hadn't heard it, he would be better off figuring the problem out by himself. In less than two minutes, he spoke.

"Tricky, Asitr, but what does that have to do with my question about time?"

"Nothing. It has to do with numbers adding up incorrectly due to a missed step in logic."

"So it's back to quiet thinking?" I asked. "This is depressing. We don't know anything, about anything, do we?"

"I'm not so sure, but I think I understand more than I know." Asitr's voice sounded tentative. "I think I understand time is one-dimensional glue, holding the world together. Wherever you are in space, time is moving forward. Not only wherever you are, but whatever you're doing, and however slowly or quickly you're doing it, time is the common thread, holding us together. Inevitable, impenetrable time, step after step, dragging us along into the future."

"Put it into numbers," I said, "and you can get published in the journals ... posthumously."

"Einstein said time was the fourth dimension." Robert added.

"He also said that time began when God moved." With a more confident voice than he began with, Asitr sounded passionate about his argument." So which is it? Is time a fourth dimension, separate from the three dimensions we can visualize? Is it a one-dimensional measurement of movement? Maybe it's the movable surface we stand on.

"Time holds the physical universe together, is the foundation of curiosity, and is necessary for self-awareness in a three-dimensional world."

"Asitr," I said. "Your theory has more abstract conclusions than Darwinism. I can't visualize time as a herd dog. Give me some numbers to hold onto."

"Or another example, like your three salesmen thing," added Robert.

"Here's a number and an example: Seventy-eight RPMs."

"A record?" I asked.

"Yes," he said. "Put it on the turntable and it spins. The outer rings of the record travel seventy-eight rotations in sixty seconds. Less than one-second per revolution. The inner grooves also travel at the same rate. The difference is in how far each groove travels in each revolution. The outer groove on the disc is almost three feet long. It races to complete a single rotation within the timeframe. The center groove begins and finishes its rotation in exactly the same amount of time, but it is meandering over a path of just six inches. What holds the whole process together? Why don't the different speeds at which the whole is moving cause breaks between grooves? Why is the music uninterrupted? By the numbers, is there a formula to explain it? Do we need one? From our ears, don't we know it's real?"

"Sheesh Kamushka," I said, "What's holding it all together is vinyl. The recording is stable because it has a firm foundation."

"That's what Asitr is saying, dipnot. He's saying the cosmic vinyl for maintaining our noise in the world is time." Robert understood Asitr's point. He also asked the uncomfortable question Asitr couldn't answer.

"If the space-time thingy is tricks of logic and math, why did your friend Enoch have to be frozen like me and Otis before he returned to earth?

Asitr didn't try to pretend he knew the answer to the question. I didn't bother to try understanding the concept. Robert's drifts into visualizing his future return was encouraging, but it didn't move the needle.

"Time may be the pliable vinyl stabilizing the song of creation," he said. "It may be the blank substance where we record our existence, but I'll smash that record to pieces if I have to, before I give up on getting out of here to see my child."

Nobody had to suggest another period of silent thinking. It was clear. The more we explored, the less we understood. We were all at the breaking point. Inside the box, there was a growing understanding that we were inadequate in figuring out a brainy solution to our plight.

Over the next two months, we spoke in spurts, but we didn't try to solve our problem. The therapy of brainstorming was over. We didn't quit. We just didn't believe we were approaching a breakthrough. I felt like an amoeba trying to predict a winning lottery number.

16

ONE MONTH IN PARADISE

THE NEAR HORIZON LIGHTENED AHEAD OF LOCK, Willa, and Dorothy. The rain slowed to a sprinkle. The solid blanket of the rampaging berserker cloud moved on. Trees above the path no longer formed an opaque barrier between sky and island. Clouds, with thin edges of light from the liberated moon, began to add texture through patches in the leafy canopy of the trail.

The path they were walking was getting wider with every step. The smell of wood smoke mingled with the clean smell of rain. Straight lines and unnatural angles at the edges of a clearing stood out, silhouetted against an opening where the sky appeared without the blockage of forest. The village loomed in front of them.

The two guides with flashlights stopped at the edge of the village clearing. "Call Sam," said the smaller of the two men, and the larger man took off in a trot toward one of the angled roofs on the left of the village green.

"The guesthouse." The remaining guide spoke in a monotone voice, leaving an ambiguous feeling of not being certain we were welcome. "The big porch. Follow the light." He shined his flashlight toward a bamboo- and wood-planked building with a thatched roof, then excused himself. "Don't wander away from the guest house."

The trio watched the beam from the flashlight disappear behind a shed, then Lock and Willa began hobbling toward the stairs of the guest house.

Behind them, Dorothy paused and surveyed the cluster of buildings and work spaces, curious about the functional reasons for unfamiliar items like a weaver's loom, a blacksmith's station, and a water tower. She was still standing in the same spot when Lock and Willa reached the stairs and noticed she wasn't behind them.

"Dorothy?" Willa didn't see her standing at the dark edge of the forest.

"I will be right back," she responded, "I forgot my feathers. They are with the secret beast in the scratching leaves."

"Wait." Lock aimed his voice toward the direction of the path. "Wait until morning. You'll get lost."

"I have eyes like a jaguar," she called over her shoulder as she sped back down the trail.

Before she returned, the lights came back on. Lock and Willa could see what Dorothy had already surveyed. Although not distracted by the common sights Dorothy saw for the first time, they were surprised to see the children standing on porches, sitting on steps in front of the nearby buildings. None of them smiled.

"This is a little unnerving," Lock whispered.

"Just smile and wave," Willa responded. "This isn't unusual, we're strangers here, and they want to know if we're friendly."

"Okay, now what?" Lock said, after having their overtures returned with vacant stares.

"We show them we know we're welcome. Help me into the guest house."

By the time Asitr pulled chairs together and found a pillow to rest and elevate Willa's ankle, Dorothy was back in the clearing. "What's she doing?" Willa asked. "Is that the *Duke of Earl* dance?"

Lock went to the doorway and watched Dorothy, head topped in bent, disheveled feathers, once again nude, stomping her way rhythmically toward an iron pot hanging over a pile of wet ashes.

She was silent, but showing both her teeth, smiling at the group of children gathered on the porch of the big house.

When she reached the blackened pot, she removed her feathers and placed them inside. Slowly, she raised her elbow and placed one hand over her mouth. Then she froze, eyes closed, motionless, looking like a leafless bush with skinny limbs twisted to resemble a human being.

"John, look at the children," Willa hobbled to the door and propped herself against the frame. "They're smiling."

"What's going on here? Look at the door to the big house." Lock pointed in the direction he was looking. "Is that Sam? The white guy with the video camera. Who is that?"

Willa pulled herself around the guest house door to get a better look at the man. He was taller than Sam, dressed in white pants and a red Hawaiian shirt.

"I don't think so," she said. "I can't be sure, with that video camera in his face, but ..."

With a gasp, Willa spun around the doorway and fell to the floor inside the guest house, scrambling to put a wall between herself and the man with the camera.

Lock dropped to his knees and tried to calm her. He saw she was scraping her skin against the rough wooden floor, biting her lip to keep from crying out, while she scooted tight against the wall.

"What is it? What's wrong? Be still," he begged, while she resisted his attempt to raise her to her feet.

When Willa was satisfied that she was as tight to the wall as she could be, she whispered, "Did he see me? Did he see me?"

"I don't know. Maybe. What's wrong? Who is he?"

"I don't want to talk about it, John. I didn't want to bring you any of my troubles."

At the doorway, footsteps creaked on the porch and Lock stood up with his fists clenched, ready to charge whatever came through.

It was Dorothy.

"That was fun." Dorothy was excited and talking fast. "I didn't want them to think I was Mahatma Gandhi. The Below People will accept me. Tomorrow when they aren't speaking with their head spirit, I will ask them where their mountain went, and why they stopped sending *Quipu*."

Lock had too many thoughts and questions dead-ending in his mind. He couldn't prioritize the conflicting sources of his confusion, so he combined his concern over Willa's reaction to the cameraman and his curiosity about Dorothy's confounding behavior, added them together and came up with a disconnected jumble of questions intended for both of them.

"Who is he? The what spirit? Mountain? The Below People? Sending *Quipu*? Are we in trouble? Mushka."

Willa pulled on Lock's belt to help lift herself to her feet. "I can explain everything," she said. "The Below People, the mountain, head spirits, the *quipu*. Later. First, you need to hide me."

"Oh, I can help with that," Dorothy chirped cheerfully. "In the morning, I will gather what you need."

Once again, a creaking sound from the porch caused Lock and Willa to stiffen. Lock inched toward the sound, picked up a chair and raised it above his shoulder, visualizing his first attack move. Ready.

Another footfall, another creak of boards, but no sign of anyone coming up the stairs to the doorway. Lock balanced his weight to the ball of his trailing foot, waiting to push off and launch himself at whoever was creeping toward the door. He slowly lowered the chair and smiled the smile of the embarrassed when the danger he imagined emerged from the porch and walked into the room.

Two children blinked at him, then smiled toward Dorothy. The first of them, a young boy, set a folded offering of red sweatpants and a yellow T-shirt onto the floor, then ran off. The second, an older girl, lay a necklace of shells and Tamamuri bark onto the pile and lingered long enough to make Lock uncomfortable. She stared at his face with the same inscrutable vacancy the villagers showed them when he and Willa hobbled past them to the guest house.

Lock stared back. His mouth was open, but no words spilled out.

Finally, the young girl turned her attention to Dorothy. "Dude, your friends are weird," she said. Then, she shrugged her shoulders and ran off down the stairs, laughing.

Dorothy covered her mouth and giggled. "They accept me," she said. "But they've given me a funny new name."

"I must have a concussion from the crash," Lock groaned. "Is it safe to sleep tonight?"

"Only if you wake up," Dorothy said. "In the morning you will know."

"I give up." Lock slumped, releasing the pressure on the muscles he tightened for his attack and addressed Willa. "You can explain this?"

"I'll try. We'll sit down in the morning and I'll try … If we wake up."

"Before or after we play our hiding game?" Dorothy couldn't have sounded more cheerful.

"Explain first, games second." Willa couldn't have sounded more resigned.

Lock found the light switch and darkened the room. "I'll stay up and watch for the camera man," He couldn't have sounded more determined.

Before the sun rose, Lock saw the red-shirted man leave the big house with a flashlight and a large satchel. He walked down a different path than the one leading to the helicopter. Lock fell asleep in his chair minutes after feeling the relief of watching the man's departure.

*   *   *

In the early morning, the sky was a golden haze. It was barely bright enough inside the guest house for Lock to make out the faces of Pineapple Sam and his wife when they jostled him awake in his chair.

"Whatcha know, big guy? What happened last night?" Sam leaned into Lock's face and rubbed his shoulder.

The cobwebs that divide deep sleep from consciousness were entangling Lock's mind, but he still was able to give a reasonable response to the question. "Hell if I know Sam. Is there coffee?"

Across the room, Willa sat up in bed, awakened by the voices. From under her pillow, she displayed a steak knife she found in the kitchen area. As quickly as she recognized the two people standing over Lock, she put it under the sheet.

Sam's wife tugged on her husband's sleeve and pointed toward Willa. "Look, she's doing it again. Didn't I tell you she tried to steal our knife at the restaurant?"

"Crap, Shori. Willa just got scared is all. Nobody's stealing anything. Let's brew some coffee and sit. I want to know what's going on."

"A lot's happened since we left your restaurant, Sam. I should have taken notes. We got stranded and rescued by ... Oh. Sorry, Willa." Lock pulled two chairs together and set a pillow on one of them. "Rescued by ... Where's Dorothy?"

"Where is Dorothy?" Willa looked through the doorway and repeated the question.

"Who's Dorothy?" Sam and Shori asked together.

Lock walked to the window and looked around the green.

Willa answered the question. "Dorothy rescued us. She's our adopted, ninety-year-old, hyperactive child."

Shori clutched Sam's arm. "She's the old bruja at the dock, Sam. I didn't know. I told her to get in her boat and go back home."

"You what? She just might try it." Willa was injured, angry, and concerned. She swung her leg over the edge of the bed and screamed when her ankle hit the floor. The pain gave juice to her concern and anger. "You what?" she shrieked again. "That lady is no bruja, you ... you bruja. Is she here or is she adrift?"

There was giggling in the doorway. Multiple gigglers. Seven girls of different young ages, all in sweatpants and T-shirts. One of them was Dorothy.

"What up, brujas?" she asked. "My posse has medicine plants for Willa. The nice shaman lady is coming to make everything better, and I have to boogy on down the road. Weaving, tinting, swimming, movie nights, books all in English. My day is all jammed up with digging my new crib. Huana is teaching me all kinds of new shit."

"Yes, I see," Lock sighed. "Shoot me."

17

TABLE TALK

W HEN LOCK HELPED WILLA TO HER CHAIR, he whispered in her ear. "Don't mention the idol."

"Don't mention the camera man," she whispered back.

"So," Sam began. "Anything familiar catch your eye last night?"

While Willa blanched at the question, Lock made sure Sam wasn't asking about the cameraman. "Familiar?" He asked.

"The big house," Sam said. "Nothing rang a bell?"

The purpose of the question was still ambiguous, so Lock walked to the window and looked at the building. "I give. What is it?"

"The officer's quarters from *Bridge on the River Kwai.* See the blacksmith's shed? Gilligan's hut. Every structure around the plaza is a replica of something from TV or movies."

"You're a quirky guy, Sam." Lock stepped out onto the porch and searched for a building he might recognize. "The outhouse?" he asked. "*Unforgiven?*"

"No more freebies. Stay awhile and catch up with our movie collection. I need some time to get your helicopter back in shape."

Lock moved from the porch and into the kitchen. "Where's the coffee pot?" he asked, then followed the question with another. "You've seen the chopper?"

"French press," said Shori. "Next to the microwave. I'll get the coffee; you sit."

Sam joined Lock and Willa at the table and asked, "What brings you crashing onto my island? My boys say you aren't much of a pilot, but the 'copter is fixable. I'm gonna go look at it after we catch up. First, what's the deal?"

"It's a three-cupper, Sam. I'll give you the short story."

The abbreviated story of events between Sam's restaurant and the island landing took only two cups. At the end, Shori left to find Dorothy, and Sam went off to check out the helicopter.

When they had the house to themselves, Lock took a deep breath. "Okay, we're alone. You can explain everything?"

18

EXPLAINING SOME THINGS

S OMETIMES, THE BEST OF EXPLANATIONS open doors to bigger mysteries. Certainly, Willa knew the doors she opened would lead to more questions than answers. In spite of knowing she was about to share a dark corner of the world better left unexplored, she unwound the tautness of her ball of secrets and hoped there would be relief in sharing them.

After squirming in her chair to get comfortable, she started with the easy answers, filling in the blanks around Dorothy's behavior the night before.

When she finished, Lock recapped. "So, when we arrived, the adults were having a religious ceremony in the big house, centered around a psycho-tropic hallucinogen called *ayahuasca*."

After a brief pause to give Willa a chance to respond, Lock continued. "Dorothy recognized who the tribe was, and what they were doing. They were communing with their 'head spirits'. She also recognized where they came from. These 'Below People', or *Urirana*, usually inhabit the land *below* the Andes Mountains, at the edge of the Peruvian Amazon. I'm guessing the mountain Dorothy referred to is the Andes?"

When Willa nodded her answer, Lock continued. "You hypothesized the Weareus people used to communicate with the Urirana using a system of colored threads and knots called a *quipu*. Do I have it right so far?"

Willa barely whispered her answer. "So far. One more tribe is represented here."

"Yes. Sam's wife comes from the oldest tribe in the Americas. The Shanahooey?"

"Sharanahua, John. Sharanahua. Her name, Shori, is the Sharanahua name for *ayahuasca*."

Venturing a guess at Willa's source of uneasiness, Lock asked, "Are you concerned about the drug use here?"

"No, not exactly. *Ayahuasca* ceremonies are common in nearly every area of South and Central America. I am concerned about abuses outside the ceremony."

Lock stood from his chair, walked to the door, and inhaled deeply. "Your concerns. Do they have something to do with the camera man?"

"God, yes."

"I'm going to have to wait to hear about them, babe. Company is coming. I think the 'nice Shaman lady' is bringing something to wrap your ankle."

19

DIFFICULTY WITH WALKING AND TALKING

A FTER WILLA ICED DOWN, poulticed, and wrapped the ankle, her leg felt better, but her mind still swelled with dark secrets. When the shaman left, she still felt conflicted. "I don't know where to start, John," she said. "Sometimes the best kept secrets are best kept secret."

Lock saw her eyes well up, and the recognition she was fighting back tears only made him more determined to hear Willa's story. He gave her some time to compose herself by walking to the refrigerator and taking out two bottles of water. After setting them on the table and sitting down in his chair, he took Willa's hand and said, "Tell me."

Willa's eyes turned from fearful tearing to icy, hardened, and focused. She looked past the window to a spot far away. "I'm crazy, John," she began. "I'm not sure, really. I don't think I'm dangerous. Not while I'm me. I'm sure I'm not insane. The camera man is insane. I can testify to that. No doubts. What I don't know is, am I crazy."

20

WILLA IN THE WEB

W ALDO KURTWOOD FINISHED HIS PACKING. White pants, sandals, and a red Hawaiian shirt sat on top of the pile inside his carry-on bag. Beneath the clothing lay a large, woven, composite-fibered bag, filled with vials of chemical agents, reagents, experimental drugs, a verbal report recorded on a micro-cassette, and a flash drive with video of *ayahuasca* religious ceremonies.

Before placing his video camera into the bag, he sat on the bed to peruse the images he recorded the evening before. He chuckled at the shenanigans of the little old woman at the *ayahuasca* cooking pot, mistaking the poses for intoxication.

On the periphery of his video, he noticed movement in a doorway. Walking his video backward, he isolated on an image of a woman's face.

"Hello, Willa," he said out loud. "Whatcha doin' here, sweetie?"

Waldo reached into the carry-on and removed his flash drive. After cutting and pasting Willa's image onto the drive, he added another finding to his cassette log. "Willa Vernon is visiting Pineapple Sam's island. Is she still working?"

He zipped the bag and took a secure phone from his jacket.

"It's Harvey," he said. "Heading to the airport."

"Harvey to the airport," came the reply.

The reply was verification the message was received. Waldo knew he would be safe from inspection of his carry-on.

When Waldo returned to New York, and entered his trip logs into the office computer, analysis began. Red-lined words of interest, names in the report, and locations were extracted. Then, the sharing process began.

Lines between far-reaching locations connected in a compartmentalized web, looking for common interest between raw data and speculative conclusions.

When the process was completed, more separated compartments, within a unified think-tank system, sent their independent analyses back to the mother system, and the spider web was complete.

Because she was a former employee of the web builder, Willa's name stood out. In the final report, she had her name mentioned with some of the most sensitive areas of the think tank's destructive underbelly.

"*Long Shadows* in Winter Haven, Florida. The *Mayan Calendar* project at Big Sur. The *Silver Book* search in Rome. Laurel Canyon's *Wild Lands Initiative*. Now, she's poking her nose into the *Soma* project. Should I go on?" Team leader Knight made his point. "She knows more than she should, and she's busy. I recommend surveillance followed by aggravated retirement."

There were no dissenters. Willa was caught in the web.

21

LIFE SHOULDN'T BE A BOX OF CHOCOHOLICS

THE QUESTION FROM ROBERT came after a long uninterrupted period of silence. "Has anyone slept since we got boxed?"

The question made me realize I'd taken the universally shared sleep cycle for granted.

Robert asked another question when no answer came. "Has anyone woke up?"

Asitr must have been as surprised as I was by the question. "I don't know Robert. I've never thought about it. You might be onto something."

"A shared dream?" I asked. "Don't go *Twilight Zone* on us, guys."

"More *Twilight Zone* than this?" Robert asked the question with incredulity. "Remember when you asked the box for hot chocolate last Christmas?" Robert didn't wait for an answer. "I felt something different when he asked."

I wasn't sure what he meant. "You felt hungry?"

"No, I felt like I should feel a chocolate craving, but I didn't. I always feel like something primal inside me is stirring when I anticipate chocolate. I assumed it was because I didn't have a belly, but now I think it's something else. I hope you don't mind if I wake up now and you aren't real."

Asitr and I must have had the same thought. "God bless you, Robert. That's so crazy," he said. "I hope it works. If this is my dream, I'll miss you too."

"Hold on a minute," I said. "I want in on this. Who says I'm not the one who's dreaming? I'll even root for the shared dream idea, but let's do it together. Wake up on three?"

In unison, we counted. "One ... Two ... Three ... Wake up!"

It was a long pause, but Robert finally spoke. "Asitr? Otis?"

"So much for the cheesy dramatic surprise of a story turning out to be just a dream," I said.

"I wonder if they have chocolate in Heaven."

The weary way Asitr asked the question made me wonder if he had given up on his steady message of believing we would eventually wind up where we were supposed to be.

Worse than Asitr's down tone was the mournful sound of Bobby sobbing. I couldn't really hear it; I felt it — I felt the pain of a child, and hopelessness followed close behind. Anything — anything to make it better eluded me, so I went quiet and tried to think constructively. My mind wouldn't let me. Over and over, like a song you can't shake loose, I heard *wake up, wake up, wake up.*

I finally understood what crazy is. Crazy is when you can't tell your mind to shut up. Crazy can drive you insane.

22

PRELUDE TO A BREAKDOWN

WILLA PUT BOTH HANDS UNDER HER KNEE for support and lifted her injured ankle off the wooden chair. "It's getting numb," she said. "I need to settle into something soft."

Lock clutched her elbow and pointed toward the door, suggesting a padded chaise lounge on the porch. "You can elevate your leg if you sit out there. Have to follow shaman's orders."

"No," she answered. "I need to be away from ears. Would you move it next to the potted palm in the corner?"

While dragging the lounger through the door, Lock spotted Dorothy, closely followed by Shori, approaching the porch. Dorothy was carrying palm branches twice her size, trailing behind her, vines dragged the sand.

"For the hiding game," Dorothy called out. "I'm sorry about the flower garden, but Shori says I can go in the woods to find the pretty things. She's very nice."

The look on Shori's face displayed frustration. "I'm going to set her down and get some rules straight, if you don't mind putting off your game playing," she said. "She apparently comes from a culture unfettered with respect for property."

"Didn't I tell you she was nice?" Dorothy lay her hiding materials on the porch and put two thumbs in the air. "Huana teaches me how to use my thumbs to say 'thank you', and now, Shori will teach me how to fetter myself with respect. I think they love me."

Lock laughed out loud, both at Dorothy's relentless cheerfulness, and the look of defeated authority on Shori's face. When he turned to share the light moment with Willa, his smile froze. Willa's expression was stark, lacking any identifiable affect. He was already worried about her; now, he was scared.

Shori motioned for Dorothy to come to her, then delivered news. "Sam says you're going to be here awhile, so let us know what you need for the refrigerator. One of my ladies is going to bring you manioc, fish, and plantain for lunch. Sam sent his boys to the mainland for American food. Anything else I can do for you?"

"Any word on the helicopter?" Willa shouted the question from inside the house.

"You'll have to talk to Sam about that. Right now, Dorothy and I are going to have a talk, then she's going to learn her alphabet from Huana."

After Lock's thank yous, Shori and Dorothy walked off past the water tower, Dorothy asking excitedly, "Sam's boys are bringing us burger doodle?"

As they disappeared behind the tower, Lock suddenly recognized the structure. "*The Great Escape,*" he said to Willa. "The tower. From the movie."

Recognizing Willa was more interested in staring at the floor than she was in being involved with what was happening around her, Lock dragged the lounger to the dark corner of the room, where Willa chose to sit, and helped her get comfortable. After he pulled a chair for himself to her side, without prompting, she started to talk.

23

FINDING TRACTION

WILLA DIDN'T STRIKE LOCK AS TIMID. In their short time together, she came across as confident, adventurous, and courageous, with a willingness to rethink, then act decisively. None of those qualities, when challenged, came with equivocation, a tendency to panic, or avoidance of necessary risk. Lock believed her qualities came from a foundation of intelligent discernment and an open mind. The kind of person who believed in "adventure with a back-up plan".

The Willa sitting next to him was a stranger, rocking and nodding her head, while rubbing the arm of her lounger as if trying to wipe the polyurethane from the bamboo. She was rambling. "Our Monday in New York ... I mean, the way things happened from day to day while, you know ... You were hunting and setting traps, and I thought it was just fun, but ... was all alive ... by Thursday evening, you didn't know what happened and neither did I, but it was on video ... God, Lock, we all have bar-codes we didn't know about, right? I thought I could explain, but I can't."

Lock had some exceptional qualities himself. He knew how to stay calm while in the confusing time zone between surprise and choosing a proportional plan of action. Rather than offer the knee-jerk lines of the panic-stricken comforter, Lock avoided the *"There, there, everything will be alright."* reaction. He rejected the movie shtick of slapping her face while shouting *"Pull yourself together, woman!"*

"Well then," he said. "Now that we have all that squared away, let's go fishing."

Willa stopped her rocking, allowed the polyurethane to remain on the chair, and muttered one word. "Schmuck."

With the runaway train stopped, Lock offered a track to start over. "Start with Monday in New York. You are talking about two years ago, right? The week of Asitr making his appearance on *The Bill Elliott Show?*"

"Yes."

"Okay, Asitr and I were in Florida, doing the show by telephone. What were you doing in New York on Monday?"

Willa's wheels grabbed onto the rails and she began to chug slowly toward her destination. After a deep breath and long exhalation, her shoulders slumped and her words came out calmly. "I was invited to lecture at a convention for investors interested in archaeological preservation. It was a gravy assignment. A vacation."

Lock offered her a chance to inhale again, asking, "The calm before the storm?"

Willa ignored the question, bowed her head, and calmed her body.

Lock thought he saw the distant focus of a séance medium in her eye, so he sat back and waited.

Foreshadowing a bad ending to her story, she quoted Mazgabar in the opening sentence of her monologue. "What could go wrong?" she asked. "All I needed to do was attend a few seminars, network at *Happy Hour*, and review an on-site field report from the archaeological team excavating the Peruvian city of Caral. I felt like a free woman, loose in the Big Apple.

24

MONDAY'S PROMISE

"**M**ONDAY MORNING, I SHOOK A LOT OF HANDS. In the afternoon, I enjoyed a lot of *Happy Hour*. In the evening, I bowed out of clubbing plans and show tickets, in favor of a date with my hotel's Jacuzzi and a night of TV. While luxuriating in my bubbles, I listened to the radio.

"TV didn't happen that night. I got hooked on a radio play. From Poison Ivy to time capsule, I listened, continually reheating the water in my tub, until the program ended, and I dragged my water-logged self to bed. Tomorrow, I told myself, I'd do something touristy."

*   *   *

TUESDAY'S TAP ON THE SHOULDER

"Tuesday morning started with room service. With only one late morning seminar to attend, I was unhurried. By late afternoon, at the open bar, my sense of carefree vacation slipped into an uncomfortable feeling. I realized I was being watched.

"A man who attended the morning seminar made his constant presence hard to miss. We bumped into each other over shrimp cocktail, martinis, and the sushi bar. He made me uncomfortable, because he didn't shy away from eye contact, but he never spoke to me. I know when I'm being hit on, but this felt different. He made me feel like I was being measured up for something else."

As soon as Willa mentioned the creepy stalker, Lock noticed her fingers start to scratch at the chair again. He set his hand atop hers and squeezed.

"That night," she went on, "I timed my bubble bath to begin with the next segment of the Asitr story. Sylvester Long's name surprised me. He's one of my favorite forgotten men of history.

"When Asitr told his mother's story, I listened with the ears of an anthropologist. My imagination began allowing me to pretend the stories were true. When Puth's story ended, Asitr made an appeal to the reality portion of my brain. He mentioned a news story on BBC.

"I was curious enough to tune in after the show. When the report actually aired, I emailed a friend at BBC headquarters. She confirmed the negotiations were real.

"My interest in the story led me to set up a new file on my laptop. I called the file *Plan B – Asitr's Nugget.* Following my usual procedure, I recorded some initial ideas to begin the project. First on my list was: Visit the *Explorers Club."*

*   *   *

WEDNESDAY'S WHOA!

"Wednesday morning, I gave my report on Caral to an audience of a dozen men. I recognized some of them. My current handler, a Harvard professor of psychiatry, and a Jesuit priest, who once interviewed me for the *Maya Calendar Project.* The stalker from Tuesday's *Happy Hour* was also in the audience.

"At the end of my presentation, I was surprised by an offer of lead chair on the Caral study team. What could I say? I was thrilled to be asked."

Willa closed her eyes and paused. When she opened them, she spoke slowly, searching her memory for details to help Lock understand her predicament. Treading water, mentally, she bought time with a travelogue.

"The city of Caral," she started, "occupies more than one hundred and fifty acres on some of the most inhospitable Peruvian desert you can squeeze between three rivers. There are thirty-five square miles of mysteries to decipher in Caral.

"Sophisticated building techniques produced a large, sunken, circular stadium, small pyramids, and impressive temples. The buildings were constructed from white granite and black limestone.

"In defiance of logical expectations, there are no indications the city was ever at war. No fortifications. No weaponry. Caral seemed to have a two-thousand-year record of peace.

"There are no hearths, no pottery.

"There's very little art. They've uncovered one gourd fragment with a depiction of the intimidating, two fanged, *Staff God*. There are geoglyphs of a long-haired man with his mouth open mid-scream. His image is repeated in multiple locations on the desert floor and in less ancient city sites just outside the city limits of Caral. The image is formed with lines of round stones, similar to the images at Nazca.

"What the city didn't have in pottery or art, it made up for in other cultural activities. Musical instruments, flutes and horns, were uncovered in temples, public buildings, and dwellings

"Mysterious, three-layered balls, with a core of textile, a middle band of hide, and an outer layer of woven vines are plentiful.

"Most challenging to the Meso-American time-line of development is the discovery of undeciphered *quipus*. Using carbon-dating, the *quipus* discovered in Caral move the prototype for *quipu* technology three-thousand years, from the time of the Inca, to a date before Egypt built its first pyramid."

Talking about the city seemed to energize Willa. She gained energy as she spoke. "So many mysteries. I had plenty to be excited about. Lots of questions, lots of ideas. Then, I met Waldo Kurtwood, my stalker.

"Waldo introduced himself as my project handler, outlined his idea of what the Caral project would be, then informed me the Jesuit priest at the presentation would be my 'co-chair'.

"After intense discussions — and fruitless negotiations — by Wednesday evening, the Caral project was looking like my new plan *B*. I know when I'm being offered an empty title, but I tried one last time to affect the project. I asked Kurtwood to give me his best offer of authority.

"What Waldo and the priest offered me was, in his words, 'The opportunity to transcend the principle of speaking truth to power.' I was being invited to, 'use power to change the truth.'

"I'm an academic," I declared. "I research. I don't fake it."

"Both men laughed. Mr. Kurtwood rattled off a list of names. While I listened, I thought of Jack VanGrada, reading the roll of *Explorers Club* heroes on the Monday night show.

"Kurtwood's dismissive delivery was offensive. 'See if you can spot any academics on this list, Missy. Charles Darwin, Thomas Henry Huxley, Pierre Teilhard de Chardin, B. F Skinner, Dr. Henry Murray, G.H. Estabrook, Timothy Leary, Marshall MacCluhan, Michael Coe, and Dr. Strangelove, himself, Herman Kahn. You're being offered an opportunity to add your name to a world-class list of icons in the universe of superior intellects. The X-Club is opening a door for you.'

"I was honored, but offended. I went to my hotel that night with two certainties on my mind. My interest in the Caral offer was gone, and I would spend Wednesday evening listening to the continuing saga of spirit jumping and devil fighting on the *Bill Elliott Show*.

"Sitting in my tub, listening, I got goose bumps from imagining the terror of Herakles, but the image of Mazgabar, hiding in Babylon's dark library, grated at my emotions the hardest. I couldn't dissociate the strategy of Satan's plan to tempt us into self-destruction from the sideways attempt of Waldo Kurtwood to lead me into the temptation of laurels over ethics.

"When the show ended abruptly, I felt agitated. I didn't understand the reason an archaeological study needed to be manipulated, and I couldn't understand the source of tension between Bill and Asitr.

"To clear my head, I went to work, setting up my laptop to video-record my ideas for the *Asitr's Nugget* project. The ringing of the phone stopped me from making a new entry.

✳   ✳   ✳

THURSDAY MORNING ENERGY

"After waking up the next morning, my laptop battery was dead, and I couldn't remember why it was set up. I had the idea I'd intended to record something to do with the radio play, but pushed the thoughts away in my excitement over beginning the *Caral Project.*

"I'm ashamed to say it, John. During Thursday's meeting, I was eagerly invested in helping to organize a plan to produce a shadow puppet play and call it research. I didn't even know I wasn't myself."

At some junctures in Willa's story, Lock moved away from strictly listening, to a mixture of hearing the details and forming conclusions. As she wove her experiences more tightly to Lock's memories of the show, there dropped a thought. It thumped, soft as a foam cup, then expanded, grew into an idea, then thudded into his psyche. From there, a feeling spread. Lock felt like he was being frozen.

The chill started in his scalp, moved through his brain, then into his spine. When the dull numb reached his fingers, he took his hand off Willa's and held it, palm out, while scooting back into his chair.

"*Shhh*, stop" he said. "Don't tell me you're possessed."

When Willa responded, she emphasized each word, one at a time. "Not. Like. Bobby."

"Like who?" Lock's tone was accusational.

"Willa reached for his hand, but he pulled it away. "I want to explain," she said.

"Who wants to explain?" Lock's chair fell backwards as he pushed to his feet and backed away from Willa. "Who am I talking to?"

"I'm the woman you dumped your angst on in the airplane to Panama. I'm the woman who was willing to follow you down a hole in Eden. If you're done with chasing devils, go. I'll handle this by myself."

Lock could see Willa was afraid, but ready to fight. He didn't know the fighters on the card, but he sensed she was fighting out of her weight class. After feeling like a failure in his own main event, he could have continued to back away, but he didn't. Because he always ran toward the danger and, for sentimental reasons, he righted his chair and entered the ring.

"Try me," he said. "Tell me what, or who, hijacked your mind."

25

HARBINGER INSTITUTE
APRIL 2, 2025

"CAN WE TALK, DOC?"
The question hung in the air until Dr. Milton realized an answer was expected.

"We're talking now, aren't we?"

"I'm talking, Doc. You're listening." Otis swung his legs out from the covers, hung them over the side of the bed, and watched himself wiggle his toes. "I'm curious. Did you ever think about all the little muscles, sinew, bones, nerves, eye-toe coordination, the switch boxes in the chain ... ever think about what it takes to wiggle your toes?"

"Not my field, Otis. What are you getting at?"

"I want to talk about your field."

Dr. Milton wiggled his toes inside his shoes, noticing the pull from his socks at the end of his big toenail. "Huh. Never noticed that before." He looked at Otis and smiled. "I wear my socks too tight."

"You do what?"

"Different viewpoints bring different views. You look at your toes and think about what makes them move. I observe my own toes, using a different sense, and I discover something that will save me money on socks. Toes are safe to talk about."

Otis looked at Dr. Milton quizzically, like he was contemplating a familiar stranger. Slowly his face slid into a crooked grin. "I see why you do it, Doc."

"Do what?"

"Listen without talking. You follow a story much better than you participate in dialogue."

The doctor leaned forward in his chair, resting his elbows on his knees, meshing his fingers together under his chin. "Here's my point, Otis. Toes are easy. Psychiatry is hard. Talking about my field, each of us with different viewpoints, would be like blurring each other's settings on a microscope. Let's narrow it down to discussing those people in my field who have *possessed* Willa Vernon. Isn't that where this is going?"

Otis Beckley's toes stopped wiggling. He shifted from exploring for a way to ask the doctor about the shadows of his profession, and relaxed, appreciative that Dr. Milton didn't need to be walked down an awkward path. He was already there and waiting.

"So how'd you know where Willa's story was going?"

"Waldo's list of hero academics was a clue. The myth of the X-Club reinforced the negative side of the clue, and the sudden personality change in Willa, after answering the phone, settled it. She's too young to be one of Estabrook's nineteen-year-old victims in the *Manchurian Candidate* program at Harvard, but from what we know now, those experiments didn't begin or end with Estabrook."

"I want to know what you know, Doc." Otis scooted off the bed, adjusting the back end of his hospital gown as he sat in the chair next to the doctor. "I've been gone twenty years, give me a monster update."

"Simply said, and truthfully rendered, Mr. Beckley, monsters still rule from their dark hiding places. If you see a creature like Estabrook, Murray, or Chardin exposed, the monsters behind them have already changed hidey-holes. Even the good guys have their research corrupted. A well-intentioned project at Stanford can reap an Abu-Ghraib event. It's project bias, not psychiatry."

"Forgive me, Doc., but it sounds like you're okay with that."

"I try to focus on one man, one mind. A good one-on-one session can reap a happy individual. For my dollar, that's enough responsibility for me. But, Willa … I'm curious about her. How did she regain control of herself? Is Willa the person you said I would help?"

26

THURSDAY'S THUD

L OCK AND WILLA SAT, Lock staring at his hands, Willa staring at the door. After a few seconds, and at the same moment, they moved their heads and made eye contact. When they did, Willa began again.

"Thursday morning, I woke up and again found the battery dead on my computer, but I was energized. The organizational meeting with Waldo was a breeze.

"The Jesuit wasn't there. 'Gone to Peru,' I was told. 'Off to secure legal rights to the information stream on the *Quipu*.'

"Waldo and I worked well together. He previewed basic conclusions we needed to include in our report on social conditions in the city. Do you know how I reacted? I went to work making the rest of the report fit those conclusions.

"By noon, I nuanced the anthropology-speak to avoid questions about the archaeological process. Before I returned to the hotel that evening, Waldo and I were architects for a model of a societal *Skinner Box*. I felt important.

"Waldo bragged our report would set wheels in motion that would bring 'comfort to our kind and control over uber-consumptive rodents.' Inwardly, I congratulated myself on being included with the elite."

Lock squeezed Willa's hand, and the effect was like pushing the pause button. After a moment, he formulated a question.

"A *Skinner Box?* What does training rats to avoid shocks and run mazes for food have to do with archaeology in Caral?"

Willa shut her eyes and sighed. She knew she was heading into territory where Elvis is alive, moon landings are faked, and economic predictions of an imminent *'trickle down'* are taken seriously. She chose her words carefully.

"Have you read Huxley's *Brave New World*, John? His fictional world is an early model of a societal *Skinner Box* design. The box where rats learn to survive is a useful toy. A demo model. Even the box B.F. built for his daughter was only a test to observe operant conditioning effects on humans. The *big box* is the end game. Continental in size. Caral is important for advancing the *big box* model."

Lock took a moment to review. "Wait," he said before Willa could go on. "I have questions."

"Go ahead."

"Caral is attractive as a *Skinner* model because ... why?"

"From what we knew, the city could have been built on Huxley's model. Caral had the Americas' oldest canal system. They connected three seasonally running rivers to a central point. Control of the water for a desert population is a powerful political tool. Control of vital resources is always top priority for the X-club.

"The priest class in Caral brewed a secret formula for making some legendary blow-your-mind juice. The kind of stuff you're willing to work yourself to death for and smile while doing it.

"The social gatherings took place in one area. It's not hard to imagine, when gathered, they heard one message, one version of the news, one set of guidelines for attitudes acceptable in their culture."

"Sounds familiar," Lock interjected. "I see how you can tie it to the novel, but how is it relevant today?

"The Caral allure comes with ease of branding. Caral will be portrayed as a city where a system of government once produced two thousand years of peace, music, and games. An oasis that bloomed in the desert because the ruling class ruled and the working class worked. For anyone wanting to escape the *Wild Lands*, trading their birthright to become *more,* for a dull, safe life as an incoherent beast of burden, Caral will beckon.

Lock's nose wrinkled at the idea. People, willing to lobotomize themselves and forever serve the permanent elite? He believed Willa was afraid without reason. "You can't just run out and buy a continent, no matter how many resources you have," he said. "You'd have to plan for ... I can't begin to imagine."

"You're right, John. Before New Caral can be established, there will have to be a demand for it. A global winnowing of the superstitious, genetically inferior, and unfortunate has to happen first. According to Waldo, in the horror of the winnowing times, the Caralist model of governance will sound like a vacation from slaughter."

Lock blanched at the words Willa was choosing, but he let her continue.

"There's a chain. There are teams fostering each link. The *misery index unit* determines the timing of events. The *McCluhan* branch beats the drum for a single world government, a single education curriculum, a unified intelligence authority, and a cloud from which all electronic information is gathered and controlled. The *Soma* team is working to perfect the joy juice. When those links are in sync, the *Lemming* team will set the world on fire.

"Survivors in the big, chaotic world of unproductive consumers will run to New Caral and beg to slave for the elite. You can bet we'll have the drugs and punishments to make 'em like it ... At least, that's what Waldo says."

Reacting to the look of concern on Lock's face, Willa lowered her voice, wrinkled her expression into a sneer, and like the sound of a recording being slowed down, drawled out the exaggerated laugh of a serial villain. "Mwa-ha-ha. Scramble, rodents, scramble."

The effort at self-deprecating humor was a hopeful act. A self-mocking act of attrition for once embracing the idea. "Like I said," she added, "we all have bar-codes we didn't know we had. At the time, supporting the project felt logically necessary.

Willa waited for a new question before she moved ahead. When none came, she asked one of her own. "Do you hear what I'm saying?"

"I think so." Lock said. "You're saying a club that began when Darwin, Huxley, and Teilhard decided to make monkeys out of men has successfully formulated an action plan of mass genocide, followed by a new *ism* based on the labors of drugged out workers, control of necessary resources, brainwashing, and the fear of an operant conditioning-based justice system."

"Yes."

"They have a lot of work to do before any of that happens." Lock's reply sounded confident, as if such scale in planning could never be realized.

"Yeah, sure, John. First they would have to convince the greatest country in the world to define itself out of power by destroying their tax base in favor of a stock market economy, write tax codes that encourage businesses to move overseas, then allow corporations to recruit cheap labor, and get the government to support that labor with welfare programs paid for by loans from foreign governments. Oh, and they would have to dumb down the schools with uniform standards that require memorizing empty facts. Perhaps, teach a Darwin-only natural science program, so the discussion of a creative God theory is forbidden. At least, we know the news outlets will always keep us informed on important things, and *Uncle* Sam would never agree to be *Sugar Daddy* Sam. Getting Americans to dumb down and exterminate themselves? Abandon self-reliance? Shred the constitution? That could never happen, right?"

Lock felt like he was being gutted. "Ouch," he said. "You don't think you could do something about all that do you?"

"Hah!" Willa jerked her head and looked at Lock with wide eyes. "Do something about it? Not me. I'm convinced I would be a Satan if I tried."

"Okay, Willa." Lock inhaled deeply and grabbed the top of his head in both hands. "Now, I'm having big trouble with knowing what you're saying."

Willa recognized she needed to calm herself down, so she lowered her voice and spoke slowly. "I'm not the movie hero who spends two hours chasing the Antichrist, only to fail because, you know, even movie heroes can't change prophecy."

Lock patted Willa's hand out of nervousness. "Fatalist or faithful, which are you?" He asked the question because he wasn't sure how much of Willa's assessments were reality and how much was from hyper fear, or worse, leftovers from a mind rape. "Why a Satan?"

"You know. God's will. Stand back." Willa pointed to the bookshelf next to the bed. "My laptop. Would you set it up on the kitchen table?"

Lock walked to the bookshelf and found Willa's computer. "You know some scary people," Lock said, as he sat at the table. "You've had your mind violated, but I'm not ready to call those eugenic maniacs the Antichrists. I don't think this is God's will. You need to give yourself some time."

"What I need," Willa growled while she painfully adjusted her leg, "is to refrain from answering the phone, and I need to kill the madman with the camera."

"Hmm?"

"The camera man. His name is Waldo Kurtwood."

When Willa's computer screen lit up, she pointed to let Lock know it was done booting. "Look in my video files for *Asitr's Nugget*. You can watch me sleep on Wednesday evening, then if you continue to watch, and don't mind me being humiliated all over again, you can see my Thursday sex tape. It wasn't only my mind being violated."

27

SLEEPER CELL WILLA

L OCK PULLED HIS CHAIR CLOSE TO THE TABLE and opened Willa's
Wednesday night video file. On the screen, behind her, was a
background of hotel art on the wall, a king-sized bed, framed by
two end tables, lamps on both tables, and a telephone on one. Her
first words spoken into the laptop, "Asitr's nugget project, visit the
Explorers Club, contact Guglielmo …" Her entry ended abruptly
when the phone rang.

Lock watched Willa, onscreen, turn her head toward the
ringing phone and, while continuing to watch the video, he asked,
over his shoulder. "You know Guglielmo Singh?"

"We've met," she said. "But it's not important. Keep watching."

The video blurred momentarily as, on-screen, Willa stood up
from the chair and adjusted her hotel robe. When she moved away
from the computer, she came back into focus, walking toward the
bed. While sitting down, she reached for the phone.

After saying hello, she sat, motionless for more than one minute. Then, she spoke. "Yes, sir. I'm very excited. I'll be sure to get my sleep in, right away."

Immediately after hanging up the phone, she pulled the covers back and lay down. As the video continued to run, she lay still.

Willa called to Lock from her corner, "If you shut it off right now, I can still deny I snore. There's a couple more hours of me sleeping before the battery dies. When the screen blinks to black, then comes back on, my Thursday night recording starts. It opens with me looking at the screen with my best blank stare until, once again, the phone rings. What follows ..."

Willa dropped her dry description of the videos and broke into sobs. Her sobs grew into gulps for air and body spasms as she fought through the words, "He ... made me ... hate ... clowns ... and white men."

"Hey, hey." Lock rushed to Willa's side. She was shaking, trembling, and hyper-ventilating. "Come on now, no hurries. Let's start with the easy stuff. Forgive the clown tribe. Don't let one bozo spoil the carload. We'll work on white men later."

Lock's silly brand of genuflection had worked to calm Willa once before. This time it took a bit longer.

"You think this is funny?" Willa screamed the words so loud it was clear she forgot her desire to be away from ears.

Lock chose silence over protestations and pulled Willa tight to him, squeezing until Willa spoke to him in a voice muffled by having her face pressed tight against him.

"It's not funny, John. Would you let go of me and see what the lady at the door wants? I think she's bringing our lunch."

*   *   *

Over flaky, sweet fishes, spicy plantain, and manioc, Willa told Lock she learned most of what she knew about the X-Club from Waldo Kurtwood's pillow talk. She asked Lock to refrain from asking further questions about the Thursday video until they finished lunch. "I might sound flaky, but my mouth doesn't want to share the food with spicy plain talk about sweet flesh and maniacs ... too confusing for the brain in the belly."

Lock appreciated the weak puns. He knew it meant Willa was beginning, once again, to relax.

After the meal, Lock found some red clover and pineapple sage in the kitchen and made tea. The two of them stirred the ice in the tea in silence, then Willa summed up what was recorded on Thursday evening.

"Between bouts of loony, vile degradation, bursts of violent sexual treatment, and demonstrations of how to cause pain without leaving marks," she said, "Waldo's drug pantry was sampled repeatedly. If you watch, you would think I was enjoying everything."

28

HARBINGER INSTITUTE
APRIL 2, 2025

"D oc?"

Otis made several observations about Doctor Milton's listening habits over the last two days. The stillness of his body in his chair, the half-closed eyes, the imperceptible breathing. Those traits made the doctor's body *tells* stand out loud against the background of his quiet demeanor.

A new *tell* showed up while recounting Willa's dark claims of knowing there was a conspiracy behind the foundations being laid for national suicide and yet another *New World Order*. Dr. Milton began readjusting his position in the chair. The adjustments grew more pronounced when Otis broached Willa's sexual abuse. Before continuing, he wanted to know if the escalating tells of discomfort were a reaction to something he said.

"Yes, Mr. Beckley?" Dr. Milton leaned forward.

"I'm skipping over the details of Willa's violation."

"Fine by me, Otis. I understand ... Sodium Amytal and deep hypnosis with a phone message trigger. Am I right?"

"That was her program, yes."

"She would be enthusiastic, even aggressive, she could never claim rape."

"Yes. Is there anything I've told you I need to clarify?" Otis still fished for a reason the doctor squirmed.

"I think I'm assimilating," Dr. Milton answered, "but I need a bathroom break. Maybe you could stretch and relieve yourself, as well. Any questions for me before I go?"

"No, nothing that won't wait. I've gotten good at waiting."

After his trip to the bathroom, Otis settled back into bed and waited. While waiting, he began to daydream about the darkest days in the box. The doldrums that followed the collapse of the brainstorming project swam to the forefront of his memories. He shivered as he began to relive the days when madness beckoned like a crafty, whispering siren.

"*Don't think about me,*" it warned. "*Don't think about me. Think about this: There is nothing but silence, and not very much of that. Where is the silent hiss coming from? Stop listening. There's nothing but silence, can you hear it? Listen. Don't think about me.*"

Otis smiled while he thought about his near-miss on the road to madness. He patted his chest, over his heart, and said out loud, "Thank you Bobby, for those twenty-eight days of silly."

Stopping in mid-step, Jarvis Douglas paused in the hallway when he heard the singing in the *John Doe* room. After listening, he ran off to inform Dr. Milton his patient was having an episode. The cheerful song echoed behind him in the hallway.

Bashing Boo Ba Bow
Bin a Bun Borse Bopen Bay
Bore Ba Bields Be Bow
Baffing Ball Ba Bay
Ba Ba Ba.

"Ah, good times," Otis drawled. "Good times."

29

D R. MILTON FINISHED HIS COMFORT BREAK, then went to his office and retrieved a bag of clothes he gathered for Otis's release. On the way back to the room, he stopped by the nurse's station and signed the daily paperwork. After reading a note from Jarvis relaying his concern about "silly singing," he left a note of his own, asking Jarvis to bring a lunch menu to John Doe's room. Before he left the desk, he looked at the activity report for the morning. "No new patients?" he asked.

"I'm not sure, Dr. Milton. There's some confusion. We're checking on it." The nurse at the station handed Dr. Milton an admittance request. I don't want to enter anything until the confusion is cleared up."

"Is this John Doe's initial report? It has today's date. Where is Dr. Abram's attachment?"

The nurse shrugged. "Hence, the confusion. What are the odds? It has to be a clerical error."

"If this is another John Doe, I want you to make sure I'm assigned the patient." Dr. Milton handed the admission slip back, but when the nurse took hold of the paper he didn't let go.

After a couple of tugs, the nurse looked into the doctor's face and tilted her head like a curious dog. "Is there a problem, doctor?"

"I want you to repeat my orders for the patient."

"Okay, sure." The curious look turned into a serious expression of worry. "I'll make sure you get him assigned to you. Anything else?"

"No. Thank you, Ms Rishard." Dr. Milton let go of his corner of the paper, returned to Otis's room, and plopped down in his chair. After setting the bag of clothes on the floor, he settled in.

The droop of the doctor's eyelids and the quiet of his body signaled the doctor was, once again, ready to listen. Before Otis continued, the doctor prompted him, without looking up, "You wanted to ask me something?"

"I didn't, no, but yes, I do. A moral question. From your perspective, why would it be wrong to kill that little pus-ball Waldo?" Otis leaned forward toward the doctor, anticipating the answer to so important a question.

"Hmm. I see." The doctor rubbed his hands together slowly before answering. When he spoke, his tone was serious. "As a doctor, I would tell you guilt would remain with you, like an infection. As just a couple of guys talking, like you and me, I'd say 'Vengeance is mine', and I'd be quotin' the Lord."

"Buzzkill, dude."

"Trying to impress me with ancient languages?" Dr. Milton returned his hands to their normal position on his lap, as if to signal his joke should end the discussion.

"Just trying to figure out if you would hold me here if I told you I was going to go kill someone."

"Don't do it." In spite of strong emphasis on the first word of his sentence, Dr. Milton spoke softly.

"Don't do which?" asked Otis. "Don't kill someone?"

"Don't tell me you're going to. Wouldn't be prudent." The doctor lifted his eyes toward Otis and stared until the dust from the murder question settled. Finally, he prompted a return to the story. "Tell me how Willa realized she was programmed. I have a professional interest."

Otis, who leaned toward Dr. Milton while waiting for his answer, slumped and sank back into his pillow after hearing the doctor's response. Averting his eyes from the doctor, he stared at the ceiling and started again.

"It was *Asitr's Nugget*. The plan-B file on her computer."

30

WILLA GONE WILD

T HURSDAY EVENING, WITH A FULL CHARGE ON HER BATTERY, Willa
signed on to her video notebook to record some ideas for the
Caral project. Seeing the *Asitr* file name in the menu jogged
something loose. She felt confused, but remembered *The Bill Elliott
Show*.

Too late, she turned on the radio and listened to the hiss of
dead air, interrupted suddenly by the ringing of the telephone. Once
again, just like Wednesday, the computer continued to record until
the battery died.

Friday morning, Willa woke up down in spirit, foggy, and
unusually sore throughout her body. "It can only get better," she
groaned, while stretching.

Rolling over to a cool spot on the mattress, she gave thanks
for a day of no meetings. Remembering checkout time was a day
away, she crowed to herself, "It's better already."

The day was brand new, but the good parts were over. Willa
began noticing things. A powder residue in her bed, granular, but

not like sugar. An unusual smell on the pillow, like kerosene and leather mixed with cotton candy. Round circles marked where glasses once sweated on the end tables. A dark stain of a wine spill on top of the blanket. She became aware of sticky wetness against her skin from areas between the sheets. After sitting up, she noticed smears of lipstick, in her color, on the headboard, and a potpourri of hairs on her pillow.

Willa jumped out of bed, feet madly running in place, hands over breasts. She was doing the *Ewww* dance, and she knew the lyrics. Her feet stomped one last time and went still when Willa bent close to her pillow, trying to identify the different hairs.

She recognized her own: black and tightly curled. Others were bright red, like a fire truck, but with a pink overtone. A few, light brown and straight.

Willa picked up the phone to call the police, but changed her mind after realizing she didn't know what to tell them. After taking a very long shower, she called the front desk and canceled her Friday night reservation.

To make sure everything was packed, she looked under the bed. The sight of the big purple clown nose caused her to speed walk out of the hotel in a confused panic.

Upon getting a room at another hotel, Willa perched on a balcony, looking out over the city. While nibbling pizza, her mood swung between anger and fear. The condition continued until Friday's dusk. Tired of dead-end questions, she went to her old standby stress reliever and opened her laptop, intending to lose herself in work.

The battery was dead. Again. Willa plugged the computer into the wall socket and accessed her video files. There, once more, was the surprise of a file called *Asitr's Nugget.* Just as before, something loosened in her brain.

Pieces of dialogue from a radio show floated into her memory. A strong sense of *déjà vu* seized her, and an electric awareness jolted her body to whirl in the chair and glare at the telephone, daring it to ring.

Incoming memories, no longer repressed, hurled themselves at her from every message storage center in her brain. The routes they traveled were all blocked by the traffic of their sudden, simultaneous release. The electric messengers were in road rage, as Willa was demanding order, and the rules of chaos wouldn't allow it.

She blacked out.

Willa didn't linger on the moment when she told Lock. She asked a question. "It was while I was unconscious, don't you think, John?"

"What was what? I don't understand the question."

"You asked me how I found out I was programmed." Willa pulled her leg off the pillow and set her foot on the floor. "I think I got everything sorted out while I was unconscious, because I remembered everything when I woke up. I didn't need to see the videos, but I did, so believe me when I tell you, I'll never answer another phone for as long as I live. If you ever wear a pinky-red clown wig, I'll burn it off your head and, most importantly, don't hang around if you can't stomach the idea of knowing I'm going to kill Waldo Kurtwood."

"Willa," Lock said. "I'm the angry, brooding refugee with supernatural experiences. You're the nerdy, sweet swaying gal in white cotton on the beach, livin' the world-trekkin' life. Surely, with resumes like ours, we can figure a satisfying way to give Waldo his bad day without murdering him."

A *harumph* and a mumbled phrase under her breath was all Willa could muster. She stared at Lock with narrowed eyes.

Lock didn't try to search for whatever dog whistle trap he might have fallen into. He was focused on his limited offer of assistance, so he returned the glare, waiting for his challenge to be accepted or rejected.

The stare-down continued until Willa understood from Lock's expression, she wasn't being asked to compromise. Lock's challenge was to come up with proportional justice.

When the silent negotiations ended, Willa asked a single question. "We're going to put him out of business?"

"For good," he promised.

Willa held her arm out toward Lock for assistance. "Give a gal a hand? I want to get to the table. We have thirty days to come up with something."

"Why thirty days?" Lock pulled two chairs together in front of the computer and crossed the room to Willa. When he reached her, she was already standing and wincing in an attempt to put weight on her foot. "Why thirty days?" he asked again.

"There are thirty days between *Ayahuasca* ceremonies, John. Get me to the table so I can show you a few things and tell you what I know. We have thirty days to ..."

Two sudden creaks from the front steps, and the heavy footfall of Sam bounding up the stairs, interrupted Willa's answer. Both Lock and Willa turned their faces to the front door.

"Hey guys." Sam walked briskly into the room and turned toward the pitcher of iced tea on the kitchen table. "Just what I need; it's getting' hot out there."

"It's good tea, Sam," said Lock. "You grow good tea herbs."

"Yeah, I need to mention that. Shori's pretty proud of her garden. She's on me to let you have it about Dorothy helping herself to the flowers. Says she trampled on the salvia." Sam opened the door on the kitchen cabinet and selected a glass. "So hey, rumble, grumble, scallywag tourists, a pox on you. There. If she asks, I got on you pretty good about it. Okay?"

Lock laughed, and let him know that Shori was in earlier to tell them about Dorothy's raid. He put his arm around Willa and braced her for the walk to the kitchen table. On the way, he asked,

"So what's going on with the 'copter?"

"Shori didn't tell you? I thought you guys were discussing it when I came in." Sam selected the chair across the table from the computer and sat down, reaching for the sweaty tea pitcher. "What else is happening in thirty days?"

The question took Lock by surprise, but Willa responded immediately. "The next *Ayahuasca* ceremony. I'd like to observe."

Sam filled his glass and tipped it to his face, nearly emptying the contents as quickly as he poured it. "Ah, I needed that. Little heavy on the clover. Next time, try doublin' up on the pineapple sage. Sometimes the subtle ingredient needs to be amplified."

"I'll consider it a tip from a master," Lock grunted, as he lowered Willa into her chair at the table.

Before Lock sat down, Willa turned the conversation back to the ceremony.

"I know a little about the vine, Sam. I know you have to wait thirty days between ceremonies. Like the tea, it's the amplification of the subtle ingredients I want to learn about."

"What I want to learn," interjected Lock, "is how long for the repairs? What's going on with the helicopter?"

Sam stared across the table at Willa, but answered Lock's question. "The engine's good. The frame? Eh. We can straighten it out here at the blacksmith station. Might take a couple weeks. Need to replace a door. Two days, maybe. I think I can get one in Panama City. The rotor assembly ... *woof.* That's another matter. It's loose. All the rotor parts need to be ordered and delivered from China. If we get them off a boat in the canal, thirty days."

Lock was surprised. "When you sold it to me, you said it was an American product."

"American assembled ... well, actually, Mexican assembled. The parts are made in China."

"How is that an American helicopter?" Lock put his elbows on the table, exhaled loudly, and dropped his head, when he realized the answer to his question was obvious.

Sam poured the last of the tea into his glass and looked at Lock like a man puzzled by a child's question. "You need to get out more, buddy. The company is American. I own a few shares myself. Anyway, bottom line is probably thirty days."

Willa raised two thumbs up and exclaimed, "Great. If we're welcome to stay that long, I can witness the ceremony."

Sam pressed the cold, empty pitcher against his brow and frowned. "Can't say, guys. Need to talk to Shori first. She's running that show." He hesitated before sending a chill to the pair across from him at the table. "I'm guessing she's going to need to talk to Wally. He's a documentary film guy. Has a contract with us to film the ceremonies. Good money. Contract runs through December. I need to check with him, too."

Deadpan expressions met Sam's statement. Sam mistook them for a sign they were waiting for something he forgot to tell them. He took a guess at the reason and reached for Willa's computer.

"Oh yeah," he said, "You wanted to know about the *Ayahuasca* additives. Let me Wiki that for you."

Willa couldn't reach her computer fast enough, but she pulled the table toward her and stopped Sam from turning the screen around. "No!" She spoke the word so forcefully, both of the men jumped. "I'm sorry, Sam. Let me close my work page. I've worked too hard to lose anything. I'm really bad about saving the work."

Sam threw his hands up and apologized. "No, no. My bad, I should have asked. I forgot you do that astropology stuff."

"Anthropology." Lock corrected.

"Sorry to correct you both," Willa said, "but I'm retired. I'm working on a novel. The first draft is for my eyes only. It's really embarrassingly bad," she added. "My first try at fiction."

Sam stood and put his chair back under the table. "Just give me an autographed copy when it's done," he said. "I'm going to find Shori and see if I can get that ceremony thing set up for you, then I'm going to fly my bird into the mainland and order your helicopter parts."

"No, please, don't bother talking to Shori," Willa hoped she didn't seem too eager for her name to go unmentioned. "I've worked on documentaries before. I know not to interfere. Your Wally guy surely wouldn't appreciate me skewing the authenticity with my presence. I withdraw my request."

Sam disappeared out the door. Two creaks later, Lock whispered, "Astropology?"

"He's got a little Yogi Berra in him," Willa laughed.

Before Willa stopped laughing, there were two more creaks, and Sam poked his head in the doorway again.

"Almost forgot. I'll be back tonight. Tomorrow, Shori and I will stay on the mainland. We have five days of restaurant reservations. There's a patch of pineapple on the north side of the island. Lop off some ripe ones, but replant the tops. Make yourself at home."

31

TRAJECTORIES

A FTER SAM LEFT, WILLA ANNOUNCED she needed a break from drama. She went to work organizing a slide show of *quipu* photos.

Lock left her to the therapy of her work and went off to clean out the helicopter.

The guest house was quiet until Dorothy spoke. "Trajectory is a funny word," she said. "It's hard to look up in the dictionary, because one letter can make two sounds, and one sound can come from two letters."

The sudden sound of Dorothy's voice caused Willa to jump. She didn't hear her enter the room. When she turned toward the voice, she saw Dorothy, on tiptoes, looking over her shoulder at the computer screen.

Dorothy continued her monologue. "Reading in English is almost as hard as counting in Shori's language."

"Oh, my. Trajectory." Willa said when she saw the thoughtful look on Dorothy's face. "What a big word for someone who just learned their alphabet this morning. Huana did teach you the alphabet, no?"

"Huana did teach me the alphabet, yes. I say yes, because she did teach me the alphabet, and yes, because she taught me this morning. I try to be clear." While trying to be clear, Dorothy put three books on the table and hopped up on the seat next to Willa.

"Huana must be a very good teacher," Willa said, "but she might want to start with some smaller words if she wants to teach you how to read." Willa spread Dorothy's books out on the table and looked for one she thought suitable for a beginning reader. "You have a dictionary, a world atlas, and an encyclopedia. Did Huana give these to you?"

"I picked them out all by myself. Huana didn't know what they were, because Huana doesn't know how to read. I'm going to teach her when she isn't mad at me anymore."

Willa realized she was staring at Dorothy with her mouth hanging open. Dorothy was staring back with a what-me-worry grin, happily picking her nose, then wiping a booger on top of the table.

"No-o-o, Dorothy." Willa's mouth closed into a tight frown. "That's not nice. It's very unclean to do that." From genuine revulsion, Willa pulled away.

"No, it's okay." Dorothy reached out and touched Willa's arm to reassure her. "Shori only gets mad if I wipe my boogers under the table. I am being a good guest. Also, I don't want to be drowned."

The tell-tale creaking of the stairs caused both ladies to turn to the door. Lock was back, sweating in the doorway, a backpack hung on his shoulder, a guitar nestled under one arm, a book clutched tight against him under his other arm. A suitcase dangled from each hand.

"Dorothy," he said wearily, "I have a book for you from Shori. You have to return the books you took from her hut and come right back here when you're done. We need to talk."

"Okay, Mr. Lockjaw, I'll be back faster than you can read Willa's *quipus*."

Dorothy snatched the books from the table and raced past Lock, leaping from one side of the stairs to the other, avoiding the creaker boards. Running down the path to Sam and Shori's hut, she shouted, "I'm on a trajectory to be there fast."

Lock dropped the suitcases and let the backpack slide from his shoulder. "There's another storm coming," he said. "Shori is threatening to drown Dorothy. Huana is crying because she thinks Dorothy is going to beat bad words out of her with a stick, and I'm getting too old to carry a suitcase full of wet clothes. To use Dorothy's word of the day, things are on a bad trajectory."

Willa motioned Lock to come sit down next to her by patting the seat. "Where did Dorothy pick up that word? She's not really reading, is she?"

Lock shrugged while he crossed the room, tossed the book on the table, and sat down. "Reading, yes," he said. "and at a very high level. Understanding? The jury's out. She's like an alien sponge. A computer. I don't know if it's a good or bad thing."

"We could use a good thing to come along about now," Willa said.

"There is good news." Lock spoke cheerfully, lifting the guitar in the air. "Two bits of good news. Grampy's guitar is okay, and I have a plan for Waldo Kurtwood. That is, if Dorothy allows our welcome to last for thirty more days. Shori is in a very bad mood."

"Sounds like our first priority is to get Dorothy under control." Willa noticed the lines of worry on Lock's brow and reached to massage the back of his neck.

Feeling a release of tension, Lock slumped forward, letting his forehead rest on the tabletop momentarily, then he raised his head. "How come, every time we talk to Dorothy, we end up with so many questions?"

"I don't know, John. Why did she fixate on a word like 'trajectory'? Will you hand me one of those napkins on the table?"

Lock gave the napkin to Willa and sighed. "It was me. At the crash site, Huana ran past me like she was being chased by a wild beast. Dorothy was sitting in the helicopter, reading her books. I asked her what was bothering Huana, and she told me Huana was afraid to learn manners the way Confucius teaches them. I didn't get to ask her a follow-up. Sam's helicopter flew over our heads and she cringed. I suppose it was memories of the ..."

Willa wetted the napkin in her glass and wiped Lock's forehead while he was speaking, causing him to pause. He stopped to watch, cross-eyed, as the trajectory of the napkin in Willa's hand ended with a wipe above his eyes. Before she lay the napkin down onto a plate of fish bones, he continued where he left off.

"Memories of the crash. Dorothy asked me where the bird came from. I told her the trajectory of the flight indicated it came from the north side of the island. She latched onto the word. Told me she was going to talk to Huana about choosing a trajectory ... Did I have something on my forehead?" Lock patted his brow to search.

"Just a little something Dorothy left on the table. It stuck to your forehead when you laid your head down." Willa snickered and changed the subject. "So, you spoke to Shori before you got back?"

"It's more like she spoke to me. She seems too angry for it to be all about the books but reassured me about the storm."

Willa craned to get a bigger view of the sky through the window. "Worse than last night?"

"Same old seasonal blow. She says it will come from the west. Our doors and windows all face the east and, with what Shori says is superior thatching on the roof, we'll stay dry all night."

Lock and Willa sat quietly, each with their own thoughts. When they spoke, they spoke at the same time, and they spoke the same words. "Tell me about ..."

Both of them laughed, and Lock gave the floor to Willa. "Ladies first."

"Is now the time to talk about your plan for Waldo?" Willa sucked her lips in and fidgeted with her fingers.

"Simplicity itself. We're going to put him in a reverse Skinner box. We can talk about it tomorrow." Lock smiled. "I think you'll agree it's poetic justice."

"I like your confidence," Willa said. "I have pictures to show you, but they'll wait. We need to solve the Dorothy problem."

"Agreed. Tonight will be about Dorothy."

"I'm okay with that. I know Dorothy wants to stay here, but she needs to learn her boundaries. Maybe a little wind and lightning will come in handy while we read the riot act to her."

Lock picked up the book Shori sent for Dorothy and held the title page toward Willa. "Shori thinks this will help."

"*Guide to the Turn-of-the-Millennium*," Willa read the title aloud. "By Miss Manners."

"Couldn't hurt," said Lock. "Couldn't hurt."

*   *   *

It was awhile before Dorothy returned from her talk with Shori. She noticed a bag of trash sitting on the porch. At the kitchen table, she saw Willa spreading peanut butter onto bread. A can of potato sticks sat next to sliced mangoes at the center of the kitchen table. Lock stood by the stove, watching water steam in a pot. On the counter, an open can of coffee grounds and the French press coffee maker waited along with Lock for the water to boil. To Dorothy, it looked like a picture of a happy new home, but after talking to Shori, she lost hope it could ever be for her.

Dorothy was returning to the guest house with a broken heart, certain Shori wasn't going to allow her to stay on the island. Until she was gone, Shori told her, the island children were to shun her.

An appeal to her friend Huana brought a response Dorothy didn't understand. "Whatever," Huana said as she ran from the room.

Dorothy walked dejectedly up the stairs without bothering to avoid the creakers. Lock and Willa turned their faces toward her at the sound, and their stern, disappointed stares sucked the last bit of hope right out of her heart. Devastated, she drooped, with eyes fixed on the floor, watching teardrops fall at her feet. "I thought I was on a trajectory of happiness," she sobbed. "Nobody loves me 'cause I'm a disaster."

Stern and disappointed looks melted. Willa moaned, "Oh, Dorothy."

Lock reached down and picked her up, patting her back as he walked to the table and sat her next to Willa. "It can't be so bad," he said. "Who wouldn't love you?"

"Shori, and Huana, that's who. And Sam, when he knows me better. The plumber. The lady with the mop. All the children, and after you know I'm a punk-ass-bitch-stupid-moron, you and Willa, too. I sorry."

Lock's temper flared. "Who called you those names, Dorothy. Don't take it seriously. Kids can be cruel."

"Shori called me a stupid moron," she said. "Huana called me a punk ass bitch and more trash talk names she learned on movie night. When I read about Confucius, I tried to teach her better. She's still my friend if I don't beat her with a stick. I sorry." Again, Dorothy erupted in tears, rocking back and forth on her chair. "I'm too old to be banished."

"Oh, hey," Lock said loudly and cheerfully. "Is that what you think is going to happen? This isn't the Weareus. This is the world. Let's eat dinner. Willa and I can tell you how to handle this. Good people can have bad moments, but we fix things. Tell us what happened."

"John, will you get Dorothy a glass of milk? She's about to have her first peanut butter sandwich." Willa slid a plate in front of Dorothy and followed Lock's lead. "The biggest problem you're going to have tonight is getting the peanut butter off the roof of your mouth."

Dorothy smelled her sandwich. "My mouth has a roof? I keep learning new things today, but I'm still stupid. That's okay with you?"

"You don't know how smart you are, girl." Willa picked up her own sandwich and took a bite. "Now, tell us what has Shori so upset."

Dorothy prodded her sandwich, lifted one corner of the bread, and pulled her finger across the gooey filling. Once again she gave it the smell test. Next, she smelled the fingers on her other hand. "I know what peanut butter is for. These people use it to kill the rats in the warehouse. I helped them with that because they don't know better than to leave them lying around stinky with their eyes popped out."

Willa pushed Dorothy's plate away from her and sat her own sandwich down, asking, "When was the last time you washed your hands?"

"Oh, you don't have to worry about that. I scrubbed with sand and water until the smell went away. I washed my whole self in the wavy water where the bird crashed down. I know about being clean to eat. I'm stupid about new things, like flush toilets. I think that's why Shori is so mad. Huana said the plumber could fix it before Shori came home, so we went to get clean."

Lock closed his eyes tight and murmured, "This doesn't sound good."

Willa braced her back against her chair and went limp. "Shori has a flush toilet?"

"Not anymore," said Dorothy. "The plumber said they would have to burn her hut down. He couldn't fix it. I sorry."

Lock turned in a circle and slapped his hands against his temples, leaving them stuck to the side of his head.

Willa tilted her head back and stared at the ceiling. "Thank God we didn't turn you loose in New York City."

"How did you … What did you do?" Lock asked the question one octave higher than his normal speaking voice.

"I learn something, and then I think I know something, then I understand I don't know enough, so I say I sorry. Huana showed me Shori's flush toilet and said it was magic for making the stinky stuff go away. It worked with poop, but it didn't make the rats go away. The more I pushed the handle the more the water spread around the floor. Those rats just stay stuck. I can tell you one thing. Dead, bloated rats don't smell better if you put them in poop water and try to push them down with a stick. The harder you push, the oozier they get and the stinkier the water on the floor gets, then …"

"Okay! I've heard enough," Willa croaked. "I've lost my appetite for rat bait on bread."

"Let's all just take a breath here," said Lock. "I can fix this with Sam." Lock pulled a chair next to Willa and whispered, "This doesn't change my plan for Waldo. We can still handle this."

Turning toward Dorothy, he smiled. "You, old kid," he said, "learn things faster than you understand them, but you know that already, don't you?"

"Yeah, I'm dangerous. Can you teach me better?"

"When we get to our new home, I want you to stay by my side until I give you your graduation papers. Deal?" Lock held out his hand, and Dorothy slapped it with her own.

"Huana taught me that slapping the hand means the same as this." She jumped from her chair and grabbed Lock, hugging him tight. "Don't worry, Mr. Lockjaw. I changed my clothes."

Overhead, the sound of an incoming helicopter caused all three to look toward the ceiling.

"At least we're already packed," Willa joked.

"Not entirely." Lock shook his head and brushed his hand across his mouth, distorting his lips before explaining. "We might have to tell Sam about the idol. I can't leave it behind."

"If you want to share the secret with Sam," Dorothy announced. "Shori will see the *quipus* on the face."

"*Quipus*," Lock said the word like a man speaking in a trance.

Willa repeated the word and followed up with a question. "*Quipus*. The marks on the face are *quipus*?"

"No, I'm not being clear. I sorry." Dorothy swung her legs over the floor, kicking her feet, and let out a frustrated burst of air. "I mean etchings. Etchings of *quipus*. Parts of them in Shori's language."

32

J ARVIS DOUGLAS'S FEET MADE LOUD SLAPS against the floor as he
ran up the hallway. His hand grabbed onto the door jamb with
a loud thump as he spun into the room. His motion stopped abruptly.
He tossed the folder containing the lunch menu onto Dr. Milton's
lap and said, "Sorry, gotta run. Trouble with Ms. Hoopla's lawyer.
He's sprayin' the nurses with a fire extinguisher. This place is a
madhouse."

Both Otis and Dr. Milton listened to the slap of Douglas' feet
trail down the hallway until, in a quiet voice, Dr. Milton murmured,
"That's kind of the point. At least in theory."

Otis let his curiosity get the better of him and departed from
telling his story to ask, "Hoopla?"

"One of our celebrity patients. Her lawyer does stunts from
time to time to keep her name in the news cycle. We call the police,
he sues, social media reports it, we drop charges, he drops his suit,
everybody gets paid. Happy, happy."

"I see some things haven't changed since I've been away." Otis peeked over the bed at the folder in the doctor's lap. "News about a new patient?"

Dr. Milton fingered the menu folder, then sailed it across the bed to Otis, asking, "Expecting company?"

"Soon. The person you're going to help is coming soon."

The doctor lifted the bag of clothes off the floor and tossed them on top of the menu. "So, you're almost finished with your story. I brought traveling clothes. Don't be concerned when you see them. White belts and polyester slacks are back in style. There's nothing in the bag that will get you attacked on the streets. That's a lunch menu underneath. Will you be staying ... on earth?"

Otis peeked in the bag and frowned. "Disco isn't back is it?"

"Just for a few dipsters. Nothing serious. Mostly auto-bus performers."

Otis raised an eyebrow. "Dipsters?"

"Disco hipsters," Milton answered. "They're harmless."

Otis looked over the lunch menu and declined. "I'm saving my appetite for a hot fudge sundae. They still have those, don't they?"

"They do. I suggest you try the low carb, with nutra-bits. Tastes like old school, before the bovine plague. Don't ask."

Otis opened his mouth, as if he wanted to ask, but closed it again and dumped the contents of the bag onto his blanket.

Dr. Milton let Otis have time to check out his new clothes, then prodded him to finish his story. "Did Lockjaw manage to get the idol off the island?"

"Nope. It's still there today, buried in sand. A lot happens in the next twenty-eight days. Head-spinning things. I'll give you the short story. It starts with Sam and Shori coming to the guest house during the storm that night, with a surprise nobody saw coming." Otis held up the shoes he pulled out of the bag and looked inside to make sure they were his size.

"They stretch," the doctor told him. "And they glow in the dark. What was the surprise?"

Otis put the shoes under the blanket and ducked under the covers with them. "They glow, Doc. I'll be damned. Why?"

"Fashion," the doctor answered. "The surprise?"

33

SKILLS IN DEMAND

S AM AND SHORI WALKED TOGETHER in the storm with what Lock called "determined strides," their faces set hard against the wind.

Willa described the sight as "ominous."

Dorothy's lip trembled and she moved to stand behind Lock. "This would be a good time for the hiding game," she squeaked.

In step, they hit the creaker boards at the same time. At the tail end of each creaking sound, the thunder boomed, as if the couple were commanding nature to roar in anger.

Standing in the doorway, water streaming down their faces, lightning flashing behind them, they looked like demons freed from hell. Even war-hardened Lockjaw shivered at the sight.

"Do you know what Dorothy's done?" Sam shouted over the constant roll of thunder.

From behind Lock, a tiny voice quivered, "I sorry."

Shori stood silent, displeasure apparent in her body language and on her face, but Sam walked to the table and motioned for

Shori to follow. Before sitting down, Sam shook water off his face and pleaded, "Somebody pour some hot coffee."

The wet couple sat, side by side, Shori frowning darkly with anger, Sam, incomprehensibly, smiling. All was quiet while Lock walked to the counter to retrieve the coffee pot.

"I have an offer for Dorothy," Sam said, while Lock poured. "Let's talk business."

Lock hovered close to the table, but Willa kept her seat on the couch.

Sam got to the point immediately, addressing Dorothy directly. "Dorothy," he began. "Huana is in awe of your ability to learn. She believes you could lead the children into understanding the world with better insight than what they're now learning on movie night. I want you to be the island school marm."

"School marm?" asked Dorothy.

"Teacher," Sam answered.

Sam let the thought sink in, then explained he wanted a teacher from a tribal background who could guide his flock "into assimilation, rather than capitulation."

"Dorothy," he told Lock and Willa, "has inspired Huana to choose a goal for her life, then plot a trajectory from where she is now to the place she wants to end up. We want her to teach our children."

Dorothy plucked at her bottom lip like a bass guitarist riffing on a string. "Not so fast, Mr. Sam," she said. "You can't just call someone a teacher of children without getting a few things straight. We need to negotiate."

Before Sam and Dorothy finished negotiating their way to an agreement, the storm passed. The only dark clouds left were the clouds of anger, still evident in Shori's cold stare.

"Well that's done," Sam said, as he stood up from his chair. He shook Dorothy's hand and told her to write up the conditions of their contract. "We'll sign it when we return from the mainland."

Shori walked to the porch, but Sam detoured to the couch and gave Willa a wink.

"Don't you worry about what happened at our house, Sam said. "We have a banyan tree, perfect for a tree house. I'm going to use the original movie version of *The Swiss Family Robinson* design. Shori and I will stay on the mainland until it's livable. Knowing my boys, I'm guessing three, maybe four weeks."

Lock walked him to the door. "I want to make a donation to the project. Maybe open a trust for future projects."

"You can start with paying to have a few septic tanks brought in. One flush toilet's not enough for an old city boy like me. Whatcha say, money bags?"

"Done deal, Sam. Thanks."

34

T HE NEXT MORNING, Dorothy drew up her contract with Sam and showed it to Lock.

1. Sam will build a school in sight of the freshwater stream that flows into the ocean.

2. Sam will choose the design for the schoolhouse.

3. All the island's children, age four through twelve, will attend classes.

4. All non-fiction books will be removed from the stinky hut and donated to the school.

5. Classes will not begin until Huana teaches Dorothy how to fish, tint, and weave.

6. Dorothy will not interact with children, other than Huana, until after Mr. Lockjaw certifies she is safe without chaperons and has received her graduation papers.

7. All the children and teachers are guaranteed the right to question or promote any concept of creation in the classroom.

8. Trash talk and boogers under the desk are punishable by one-week suspensions.

"Better than a lawyer," Lock commented, after reading the document.

"I'm happy to see Shori and Huana got to have some say," Willa added. "Try to discourage boogers on top of the desk as well."

"Gotcha," Dorothy said. Then she took off running to her first class in weaving.

"Don't forget our meeting tonight," Lock shouted as she ran through the door.

"Gotcha," she repeated, while jumping from side to side down the stairs.

After watching Dorothy meet Huana, join hands, and jump together in a circle of celebratory laughing, Willa sighed. "Why didn't we have children, John?"

"We met too late?"

Willa nudged his arm. "You know what I mean. We would have been good parents."

"I think maneuvering through the terrible-twos and the insane teen years is a little different than enjoying the blooming-nineties." Lock kissed Willa on the forehead. "We didn't plan our trajectory, but we're doing okay."

*   *   *

The shipment of refrigerator food arrived late in the morning. Along with the food was a crock pot. When Dorothy returned in the afternoon, the smell of pot roast filled the guest house, and Willa was bombarded with questions about "smell good" recipes. Dorothy announced she was going to make a book with "all the recipes I like to smell."

Lock reminded her she had commitments to other projects as well. "In particular," he said, "tonight you are going to teach us what you know about the *quipu* on the idol's face."

"Before we get into that," Willa interjected, "I have more *quipus* to show you."

"The pictures on your computer?" Dorothy asked. "I think they are something, too."

After dinner, the table was cleared, and Willa began her slide show.

Before allowing Dorothy to investigate the pictures, Willa gave a brief review of what she was going to show. "I have one photo of a *quipu*, rumored to have phonological and logographic information. It's owned by a family in Naples, Italy. I say 'rumored', because the family who owns the *quipu* allowed it to be examined, only once, by a team of Jesuit experts. Most scholars still hold to the belief *quipus* are useful solely for numerical storage."

"Well, that's just so much mushka on the truth," Dorothy chimed in. "I was trained in the teachings of the first *quipucamayac* of the Weareus. He learned his skills from a *quipucamayac* of Shori's tribe before the Quecha became big. Some *quipus* do have words to read. You can tell the scholars you know this from Dorothy, the last *quipucamayac* of the Wearus."

"Somebody translate, please?" Lock begged. "I'm resigned to never knowing what's going on, but I refuse to quit trying."

Willa answered, "Dorothy is saying she is trained in the oldest traditions of interpreting *quipus*. She is disputing academic belief in the Quechan — meaning Incan — origins of the *quipu*, as well as the teaching that *quipus* don't contain literary, along with mathematical, content."

"Thanks," Lock said sheepishly. "Now, I'm caught up."

"Alright, John no more questions. You too, Dorothy. Look closely at these photos. Don't say anything until you see everything. I don't want to influence you."

Dorothy pulled herself up on the table until her toes were the only remaining part of her body touching the chair. She placed her hands under her chin and squinted into the computer screen, uncommonly still, waiting for Willa's slide show.

Some of Willa's pictures were generic shots of deciphered *quipus* containing lists of trade goods and census counts. Six photos were pictures of the Caral *quipu*, taken from different angles and poses. One picture was a *quipu*-like image of a ceremonial necklace. A picture of a large wet-mop was included.

When the slideshow ended, Willa asked Dorothy to show her which of the items were not *quipus*. She took the mouse from Willa's hand and indicated the necklace and the mop.

Willa congratulated her for being correct and deleted the images.

"Ooh," Dorothy crooned. "I would like to have this machine to teach my classes."

Willa ignored the comment and gave Dorothy new instructions. "Show me all the *quipus* that have only numbers. No words or letters."

"How about *quipus* with sounds?" Dorothy asked. "Do you want to know which ones have sounds?"

"Sounds? Yes, I want to know about the sounds, but first I want you to tell me which ones have only numbers."

Willa ran through the slideshow again, and Dorothy poked her finger on the screen each time a numeric *quipu* came up. Willa deleted each picture as Dorothy identified them.

When the slideshow reached its end, Willa leaned back in her chair and clasped her hands over her mouth. Talking between her fingers, she spoke softly. "What we have left is seven photos of only two *quipus*. The *quipu* in Naples and the *quipu* from Caral. This is a remarkable moment, John. Dorothy has the ability to dust the cobwebs from myth and reveal more cultural history than anyone since Herodotus."

Dorothy slid back to her chair, pulled her knees to her face, and began rocking.

Lock turned the screen to get a better look.

Willa did a drum-roll on the table and announced, "This is the only complex language known to man, recorded in a 3-D system. Dorothy is the only person alive who can read all of it."

As soon as they both turned toward Dorothy, their smiles turned into words of concern. Dorothy appeared to be in distress.

"What's wrong?" Willa asked. When no answer came from Dorothy, she asked Lock, "John, what's wrong?"

Lock knelt by Dorothy's chair and touched her on the shoulder. "Did you see something bad?"

"No, I'm trying to think," Dorothy answered. "I need time. Maybe I can't read all of it. The *quipu* etched on Mr. Lockjaw's shiny beast is part of this puzzle. They all belong together, but they're different. One hangs from a stick, and I can't read the markings on the stick. One hangs from a cord made of knots. The shiny *quipu* has no colors and hangs from beads of mixed sizes. One of the *quipus* is in two languages. Two of them have writing from three languages. One of them has symbols not found in any language I know. Two of them have numbers in a trinary counting system. All of them have numbers in a binary system. From one to the other, they are all mixed up, but put together, I might be able to read the three of them separately. I don't have a lot of time. I'm starting a school for the children. Maybe a good future for children is more important than trying to be clear about the past. If you want me to read them fast, I sorry."

Willa broke into a half smile. "It's hard to believe, but I think I followed that."

"Hold on a minute." Lock slapped himself in the forehead. "I think I'm starting to understand it now. These three *quipus* are like the Rosetta stone?"

"Yes, but no," Dorothy groaned, "I try to be clear."

Lock and Willa stared at each other across the table, their bodies still, their faces frozen. Dorothy bowed her head but watched her two friends through upturned eyes, while on her lap, her fingers fumbled together.

After the silence, Lock stood up and looked at the pictures on the computer again. "With everything else, important things," he placed a hand over Willa's, "do we have enough time? Thirty days isn't very long."

"Twenty-eight days." Willa caught Dorothy's gaze with her own, and asked. "How long do you think it will take to teach me how to read the *quipus*?"

Dorothy pulled again at her lips and waved her head from side to side while thinking. Finally, she shrugged and put her palms up. "I don't know. How long did it take Herodotus to dust the myth off his *quipus*?"

35

KILLER BEES IN A BOX

O TIS WALKED INTO HIS BATHROOM, carrying his clothes with him, talking as he went. "You know, Doc, those three people at the kitchen table in Panama had a plateful of issues to tackle. In the box, we had only one thing on our mind. For our own sanity, we needed to find a distraction.

"It was Robert who started us on our way. He was surrendering hope for his goal of escaping the box. He replaced his loss of hope with a plan to reach out beyond his prison to touch the life of the soul he brought into the world.

"I don't know how close Asitr was to losing his mind, but I felt mine was out of my control, until Bobby's voice shattered my world of loud silence. 'I'm ready,' he told us. 'Let's make a Christmas album.'

"My depression was so deep, joyful noise wasn't any more appealing than loud silence.

'Why?' I asked.

'I've decided to pass something along to my child.' The way he said it had the sound of a dying patient, getting his affairs in order. 'I want to share a moment when I made people laugh on purpose, and I didn't get mad.'

"What else could we do? Robert needed us. The formation of a space-traveling boy band, *The Killer Bees*, became official on the same day Lock and Willa began to plan for Waldo's bad day. Both quests would end twenty-six days later.

"It took us two days to satisfy Robert's rules for the use of the letter 'B', but on that first day of band practice, it was fun. We started with Jingle Bells.

Bashing Boo Ba Bow
Bin a Bun Borse Bopen Bay
Bore Ba Bields Be Bow
Baffing Ball Ba Bay
Ba Ba Ba."

From the hallway, Jarvis heard the singing from the bathroom in the John Doe room and peeked in, noticing the empty bed. "Everything dandy candy, Doc?"

Dr. Milton lifted his head and waggled his fingers at his aide. 'Dandy candy,' he repeated." With confirmation things were okay, Jarvis retreated.

Otis leaned through the doorway to the bathroom, buttoning his new shirt. "Beg your pardon?" he asked.

"It was nothing. The shirt's a good color on you."

"Befitting a boy-band star?"

Dr. Milton stiffened out of his listening position and asked, "This role-playing therapy, it's sometimes an effective therapeutic tool. What effect did it have inside the box?"

Otis walked to the widow, smoothing the wrinkles in his new shirt. "Therapy, Schmerapy, Doc. It was fun. Boy, did we need fun. Even our failure at three-part harmony was something to laugh about. Working on Bobby's project was a diversion, But, for Bobby, it was serious business.

"We knew the Christmas album was his attempt to make a gift for a child he felt he would never know. To make it safe, memorable, and forever cherished, he grounded the project in the beauty of harmony, the humor in contortion of the consonants, and the love of the Christmas season. 'I want to pluck the right strings. No misses,' he said.

"After learning his system for using the letter B, we all learned several hard lessons.

"We learned a lesson in too much familiarity. After repetitious rehearsals, nobody wanted to record *Bingle Bells*. Constant repetition sucked the fun out of the song. We began to drag when we sang it. 'Sounds like a funeral dirge,' Robert said.

"We learned that even if you could carry a tune, it didn't mean you could sing three-part harmony. A tin ear for harmony can't be overcome.

"We learned the sacred songs of Christmas lose their power when you distort the words. *Bo Boby Bight and Bibent Bight* ... 'nuff said.

"We also learned that harmony can come by playing to individual strengths and the universal desire to sing along, talented or not.

"In the end, musical director Robert McKinney produced an album of sing-along songs with three solo performances mixed in. The songs were celebrations of the four seasons on earth. The discombobulation of consonants for the bubbly bravado of the letter B brought to bare the birthing of banal but boisterous balladeering in a box of boredom.

"I'm not saying every song was strong. *Bain Bops Beep Ballin' Bon By Bed* was a little too *Lawrence Welk*-y, but the beat box version of *Bubberbime Blues* just bopped, baby.

"Then, there was Robert's solo. Robert, himself, wrote his own review. 'Smooth as Perry Como, as heart-felt a rendition as you could expect from a twelve-year-old Elvis.'

'Uhuh, uhuh, Uhuh, Uh, *Best Butts Boasting ... By a Bopen Bire.*'

"Yeah, the song lingers in the mind.

"Old, serious, Asitr suggested a warning on the album label. 'Don't try this at home when gassy.'

"After twenty-six days of silliness and singing, Kae'Lairy suddenly shut our windows to the outside universe. We supposed he was blocking our music from his ears.

"Later, we discovered his ears were tuned to radio signals from earth. From an island off the coast of Panama, the harmony of three people working in ways that called upon their individual strengths was concluding.

"The results, like our own, were organized, but arrhythmic, with discordant passages and quirky solos. Like *Grateful Dead* guitarist, Bob Weir once said, "Play your mistakes and call it jazz."

"The jazz in the Panamanian composition ended with a distress call on ham radio. The composition ended with crazy Kae'Lairy back on earth."

36

PROJECTS

BOREDOM SET THE TEMPO FOR WILLA during her days of healing. Lock fashioned a crutch for her, and the shaman lady announced she was cured on the third day of treatment. Her ankle was black and blue, but the swelling was gone. Six days later, she tossed her crutch and moved around with only a slight limp. During her crippled, limping days, she spent the mornings and afternoons alone.

Lock spent most of his time working to prepare the helicopter for the arrival of the parts. He wanted to make sure it would be ready to fly before Waldo Kurtwood returned. "The only thing out of my hands," he told Willa, "is the arrival of the rotor assembly."

"I've noticed some of Sam's workers hammering away in the blacksmith station," Willa said. "How are they doing?"

"Most of that activity is for the tree-house," Lock replied. "The guys I'm working with are a little odd. Not friendly. Not unfriendly. Efficient, independent, and aloof. I think we'll be okay."

After one week of study with Huana, Dorothy was prepared to switch projects. She brought home a thatched palm mat she made for the entryway on the porch.

"I have time to read," she announced.

At dinner, she presented Lock and Willa with a rug she made from scratch. "I twisted the fibers, I dyed them, and I wove them on a loom. It looks just like everybody else makes them. Next time, I want to make my own design."

Willa gushed over the colors and the precise weave. "I love our time together at the dinner table." She ran her hands over the fibers. "I'm going to hang it on the wall."

"Dinner is a good dime to dalk wid you," Dorothy muffled, while removing a fish bone from her mouth. "Fishing and walking are good times for talking with Huana,"

"How are things going with Huana?" Lock paused when he asked the question, his fork halfway to his mouth. There was still a little tension in asking Dorothy how things were going.

Showing she was spending too much time with the thesaurus, Dorothy answered, "Huana is impeded in comprehending reading, but she is mitigating my goal of learning to slow down. She edifies me to tamp down my excitability, and ameliorates my pilgrimage toward eradicating impulsive whims, thereby facilitating the acquisition of my graduation papers. I wish I could take her sadness away."

Like an old married couple, Lock and Willa were, more and more, speaking the same words at the same time. "Her sadness?" they asked in tandem.

"She misses her sister, Caspi."

Once again, in unison, "Her sister?"

"Yes, I can show you where she lives. Huana says they don't talk anymore. Caspi is just another adult in the tribe. I think Huana likes to talk with me because she misses her sister. I'm like food in a belly for filling an empty space, but I try to fill the space in her heart."

"You're a good friend, Dorothy. Tomorrow, I think I'll be able to take a long walk. Will you show me around?" Willa looked at Lock. "Maybe John will come with us."

"Just tell me what time, girls." Lock stabbed another forkful of fish. "We can meet on the porch."

37

WALKING SAM'S ISLAND made it feel larger than it was. Like a river, paths to different areas meandered through the vegetation. No pathway could be called an avenue.

The next morning, after meeting on the porch, Willa asked Dorothy if she knew the way to the pineapple patch.

"Yes," she said, "we should take the path going east. When we see the banyan tree, we should take the path on the right, going west, and follow the wide path to where Sam keeps his helicopters. The pineapples are growing at the end of the second trail after the path going north."

On the first hike, they followed Dorothy but made it only as far as the banyan tree. Willa sat down and admired the progress already made on the tree house. When she tried to stand, she announced, "I'm sorry, I should have kept my crutch. I need to go back."

"Tonight is movie night," Dorothy told her. "You can sit on the porch and see the movie. You won't have to walk."

"Your very first movie?" Lock asked, while helping Willa to her feet. "What's showing tonight?"

"*Bride of Frankenstein.* Huana says I'll be too scared to watch."

"Do you think you'll be afraid to watch a scary movie? In America, we have a secret for taking the scariness away." Willa winked at Lock. "We eat popcorn and scream at the scary parts, pretending it's real."

"All right, then." Dorothy jumped in the air in celebration. "What is popcorn? Can Huana eat and scream with us?"

Before the movie began, Willa worried she wouldn't have enough popcorn to share with the audience. By the time the movie started, she knew her fear of committing a social *faux pas* was unfounded. The only tribal adult at the showing was the man who operated the equipment.

The children gathered around the guesthouse porch and joined in the fun. Popcorn turned into edible missiles, and screaming was enjoyed by all. The high moment came when Ms. Frankenstein, with electricity coursing around her, opened her eyes and spread her fingers like an eagle ready to grab a victim in her talons.

During the screams, Huana shouted, "Oh, no! It's Shori!"

Those laughing screams were the loudest of the night.

After the movie, Lock mentioned the moment to Willa. "I don't think the children care much for Shori ... and about the man who brought the equipment ... I don't know. Are we missing something here?"

Willa never visited an Urirana settlement, but she knew their history of rape, conscription, concubinage, displacement, and ecocide. She guessed Sam saved this band from the genocide of the Fujimori government. "It's just their way, John. There are less than two thousand Urirana left in the world. The adults survived hard times. The children seem normal."

"A little too normal." Lock looked at the porch full of popcorn litter. "I think they left more behind than they ate."

Dorothy helped clean up the popcorn, and when everything was swept up, she sat with Lock on the porch, watching the rain clouds forming overhead. "I like to see what the light does to the sky," she said, distantly. "First you get the twinkling of the stars, then you get the wrinkling of the clouds when the moon shines through the skinny places. Tonight, I forgot about the sky and watched light flickering, captured on a screen, making moving pictures. I know forever, from now, sometimes, when lightning flashes, I will think of genius men. Fools who play in God's world, taking parts from what they could not create and making monsters. When I think of Shori, I'll laugh, but I don't know. Should I laugh? Maybe scream, 'cause it's scary. Why am I sorry for her?"

"Are you being philosophical, or giving a movie review?" Lock felt the first drop from the night's rain but continued to look at Dorothy, waiting for an answer.

Several drops hit Dorothy's face. The pace of the splashes continued to quicken, then she closed her eyes and answered. "I'm only happy-sad, because I think I want to enjoy the evening a little longer, but now ..."

A loud crack of nearby lightning caused them both to jump in their chairs, and the heavens emptied their pent-up buckets. In the short dash to the safety of the guest house, they got soaked.

"Hooga mushka," Dorothy exclaimed. "I felt it coming, and it got me anyway."

38

AFTER THE FUN OF MOVIE NIGHT, new routines developed for everyone in the guest house.

At the end of each evening meal, the girls began working together on deciphering *quipus*. Lock excused himself from the sessions. I'll wait until Willa can give me the plain-talk version," he said.

For Willa, the sessions with Dorothy were exciting, but the rest of her day was a continuous cycle of waiting for the evening. The mornings were spent doing light chores and reading. Soon her ankle felt it was near one-hundred percent, but Willa slipped into tropical habits. She bridged her solitary mornings and afternoons with mid-day siestas.

Lock spent three more mornings assisting Sam's men in straightening the frame on the helicopter. When the job was finished, he was left waiting for the delivery of the door — already several days late — and hoping the rotor assembly would be on time. Waiting and hoping weren't enough for him. He began using old skills to fill his days. Mapping Sam's island, although he had dual intentions, became his solo project.

Dorothy had enough projects to fill her entire day. Each morning, she fished with Huana and discussed curriculum for the new school. In the afternoons, she worked the looms, making cloth squares with distinct designs. After dinner, she joined Willa in muddling through the mysteries of the three *quipus*.

This pattern lasted for just over two weeks until, in synchronicity, all three made announcements after a breakfast of yam pancakes and bacon.

"I have my school curriculum worked out," Dorothy said. "I'm going to show all the children the maps in the world atlas, then ask them to show me where we live. Next, I'm going to tell them they can only find our island if they use the right tool. The right tool is knowing how to read.

"Huana will teach them the alphabet, then we will read together. Run, Spot, run. See Spot run. Look at pan. Pan is hot.' When they start to sound out words, we'll look for Panama on the map. When they see how big is the world, we will explore it together, because I don't know either. Our imaginations will want to hear stories from people who live in other places and other times. Only then, while we are learning together, I will say I am a teacher."

While Willa was congratulating Dorothy for coming up with a thoughtful teaching plan, Lock walked to the bookshelf. "I think I have something to help you out," he announced.

Pushing away the dishes in front of Dorothy and Willa, Lock laid his maps of Sam's island onto the table. Dorothy immediately recognized most of the features on the maps.

"Can I use these in class?" she asked excitedly. "Can I sit on the porch and study them? I want to play the hiding game and see if my class can find me by using the map tool."

"Sure," Lock said, "they're a gift for your new school. Look on the back page."

Dorothy turned the papers over and squealed. "Ooh wee! Thank you, Mr. Lockjaw." She flashed the back page at Willa and ran to the porch, waving the maps in the air.

Willa didn't have enough time to focus her eyes on what was written on the back, so she asked Lock, "What did you do, John? Propose marriage?"

Lock laughed and sat next to Willa. "I did sign my name to a contract. I wrote three words: *Dorothy's graduation papers.*"

"So, you're done mapping?" Willa took Lock's hand and leaned forward, speaking low so Dorothy couldn't hear. "I want you to spend the morning with me. I want to know what we're going to do about Waldo, and I want to tell you what we know about the *quipus.*"

From the porch, Dorothy yelled to Lock, "I don't see the tower behind the warehouse, Mr. Lockjaw."

Lock shrugged his shoulders at Willa. "Bring me the map, and show me what you mean."

Dorothy dashed back into the room, setting the maps down in front of Willa, placing the four pages together, aligning a map of the entire island. "This is the warehouse," she said, putting her finger on a small black rectangle, "and this is where the tower is." She put her finger directly on the edge of the rectangle. "Maybe you didn't see it because the vines grow all the way to the top."

"Thank you, Dorothy. I'll check it out this morning. If I see a tower, I'll add it to the map."

Dorothy gave two thumbs up and skipped to the door. "Tomorrow, I will show Huana the maps. Today, I'll tell her about my graduation papers."

Before Dorothy leaped from the porch, Willa picked up one of the maps and pointed to some long rectangles. "What do these represent, John?"

"Longhouses," he said. I think it's communal living quarters for families."

"And these circles on the other side of the page, what are they?" Willa put a finger to her cheek and returned the section to its place.

"A cluster of small huts. I think it's a female-only living section. They stay busy working looms and brewing some sort of smelly drink."

"My ankle is feeling really good, John. Will you show me these places today?"

"If you're feeling good enough to walk and talk, I'll give you the plan for Waldo on the way."

39

LOCK REACHED FOR WILLA'S ELBOW on the way down the steps. "Do you remember the path Waldo took when he left that night?"

"No, John. I was hiding." Willa tested her ankle before descending the stairs. "I can walk fine. You don't have to treat me like a cripple anymore."

Lock removed his hand from her elbow and slid it down her arm, "Not a pity hold," he said, while wrapping his fingers around Willa's hand. "I want to."

Willa squeezed a thank you for the gesture. "You lead, I don't know where we're going."

"Due east. The narrow path. It's the long way around to the places you want to see, but I want to show you how we're getting Waldo off the island."

As the ocean came into view, Lock mentioned he believed the path they just walked may be the only straight path on the island.

When they got close enough to see the small dock, Willa pushed large fern leaves away from her face and added, "The narrowest, too, I hope."

"Look to your right," Lock pointed to an opening on the other side of the large fern. "That's another path. It's wider than this one, but not by much."

"Where does it go?"

"Are you still good to walk?"

"Spring chicken." Willa did the James Brown heel-toe shuffle on the sand. "I'm fine," she said.

"First, check out the dinghy tied to the dock. Notice anything?" Lock led her to the dock's end and pulled the rope securing the small boat to the piling. He didn't wait for Willa to answer, he told her where to look. "The dinghy has a name."

Willa's eyes drifted to the wood-burned lettering on the side of the boat and gasped, "The *Wally K.* Where did it come from?"

"I'll tell you while we walk." Lock pointed to the slightly wider path next to the fern.

"Getting conversation out of the boys working with me on the 'copter is like pulling teeth," he began. "I did learn a couple things about the man they call Mr. Wally. When he arrives for the ceremony, he flies in. He lands his helicopter on the north end of the island where Sam keeps his own birds. Last month he unloaded two satchels and rowed that dinghy to the dock."

"Why does he go to all that trouble?" Willa looked toward the north and stumbled when she lost her focus on the path.

Lock felt her fall into him and chuckled. "I think you answered your own question. I rowed his boat to the dock yesterday, to check out the distance. It's a short trip by boat. From the dock, a straight shot down the narrow path to where the *Ayahuasca* ceremony takes place. It's a faster option than walking the trails."

"Where does this trail lead?" Willa asked.

Lock stopped and pointed. "Around the next turn is the warehouse."

"Where Dorothy gathered her rats?" Willa folded her arms and blanched. "I'm not going in."

"I've been inside once, hoping to solve a mystery," Lock said. "Waldo arrived with two satchels, but I watched him leave with one."

"We can go, then?" Willa stood in front of the warehouse door, looking at a well-traveled path curving east in one direction, and south in the other. "Which way?"

"We take the curve to the east. Eventually, it will take us to the long houses." Lock held his forefinger up and reminded Willa, "First, I have to look for Dorothy's tower."

The vegetation was thick around the back half of the building. The palmetto clusters were old growth, with stalks too close together to maneuver through them. Impenetrable, overlapping branches of sharp-edged leaves ensured anyone who tried to push through would be stabbed and sliced, no matter which direction he tried to move.

Behind the palmettos, taller bushes and trees, covered in vines, poked their heads above the wall of green guardians, but approach was impossible and visual clarity was difficult. Neither Lock nor Willa spotted a tower.

"I'll bring Dorothy by later," Lock said in frustration.

"How far to the longhouses?" Willa asked. "I feel like the rats are watching us."

On the way to the longhouses, Lock revealed his plan for Waldo. "The capture will be simple," he declared. "I'll wait at the boat dock and knock the living slobber out of the clown. Next, keeping it simple, I'll truss him up and row him to our helicopter."

"And the Skinner Box?" Willa was on board with the slobber knockin' and trussin', but she didn't guess the "poetic justice" simplicity of Lock's Skinner Box plan.

"We fly him to Eden, warn him about the poison ivy, and tell him goodbye." Lock smiled, waiting for the whole picture to form itself in Willa's mind.

"Oh, my God, John. Boxed in. His Skinner box turned inside out. All the resources he needs are in the wild lands. Waldo's out of business."

"For good," Lock added. "Second thoughts?"

Willa stood stone-faced, her fingers tapping on her leg. "Yes, I do." Willa paused on the trail. "We have nine days to fix the copter. What if?"

Lock reached into his pocket and displayed a key for one of Sam's helicopters. "I let a devil get away once. God forgive me if I let it happen again."

The walk to the long houses was silent until a noise caught their attention. They both stopped walking and turned toward the sudden sound. In unison, they asked, "Do you hear that?"

"Sounds like an air conditioner starting up," Willa replied. "Who has air conditioning?"

Lock didn't answer right away. He stared in the direction of the noise; his puzzled expression gave away his confusion.

Finally, he answered. "I should have brought the maps. I thought it came from the direction of the warehouse."

"Nobody has air conditioning here." Willa cocked her head and listened, trying to pinpoint the location of the sound in the muffled maze of trees. "I don't know what it is. Might be a boat on the water.

"It's not the warehouse," Lock said. "There are two windows in the warehouse: one on each side of the door. Neither of them have air conditioners." Lock gave up trying to figure where the sound came from and repeated himself. "Should have brought the map."

✳   ✳   ✳

From photos, Willa was familiar with Urirana longhouses. "This looks authentic," she remarked. "Communal homes, temporary framing, and rain tight thatching. Sturdy enough to suit a semi-nomadic lifestyle. It's curious, though. Their craftsmanship is so much more evolved when they work on Sam's projects."

"The round huts for the women are much better built," Lock said. "We need to walk through the plaza here if you want to see them."

"Are we welcome?"

Lock waved to one of the men he worked with on the helicopter, without receiving a response. "Welcome? They won't even acknowledge us. It's the same everywhere on the island."

"These are traumatized people." Willa smiled at a group of three children sitting together on a hammock. All of them returned her smile, then put their heads together in a conference of private whispers. "How is it in the woman's *agllawasi*?"

"The what? Is there any anthropology talk that uses English?" Lock pointed to a path heading east. "If you mean the round huts, we go that way."

Willa walked toward the path, but questioned the direction. "On the map, you show the huts to the west of the longhouses and, just so you know, we don't use English because the cultures who name things don't give a rodent's behind if you would prefer they speak English."

"My apologies for being insensitive to Urirana tongue twisting," Lock replied. "And just so you know, if you want to go west on Sam's island, you usually have to start in another direction. Are you getting snippy because your ankle's acting up again?"

"My ankle is fine. I'm fine. There's too much going on in my head. Waldo, the out-of-place *agllawasi*, the *quipus*, and worrying about the helicopter parts." Willa smiled, unconvincingly.

*　　*　　*

The odor of *chicha*, fermenting in clay pots, reached Lock and Willa before they reached the *agllawasi* area. "Smells nasty," Lock commented.

"It may taste better than it smells," Willa suggested. "It's made from dried corn, water, and the saliva of virgins. The Quecha have been drinking it for over a thousand years."

"I'll stick with bourbon." Lock walked ahead of Willa until they arrived at the plaza where the round huts came into view, then he stopped and waited.

Willa caught up and reached for his wrist, pulling him away from the opening. "I don't want to go in, John. I want to talk to Dorothy first."

"Something's wrong," Lock replied. "I want to know what it is."

"It's nothing," Willa insisted with another tug on his wrist. "This area is Quechan culture. Incan, if you prefer. Urirana living a Quecha lifestyle is an anomaly. They don't mix well. You know how anthropologists get all hung up on anomalies. With everything else going on, I'll have to triage my curiosity to the back burner."

"And the front burner?" Lock asked.

"I have two pots boiling," Willa answered. "Keeping Dorothy in the dark about Waldo is important to me. Let's go where we won't be overheard, I'll update you on the *quipus*."

40

O N THE ROUTE FROM THE AGLLAWASI TO THE GUEST HOUSE, Willa broke down the academic shorthand into plain English. Of the three languages mixed among *quipus*, Willa emphasized the language Dorothy believed Shori might understand.

"It's an agglutinative language," she said, "with an SOV structure and phonology nearly identical to Shori's Sharanahua language. Surprisingly, the SOV structure and phonology is similar to the Weareus language as well."

Lock didn't ask questions. He waited for Willa to interpret. His patience paid off, eventually.

"In a nutshell," Willa summarized, "The three-word only rule of the Weareus language, alongside sharing an identical phonology with Shori's Sharanahua tribe, means ..." Willa paused to compose her explanation and emphasize the importance of what she was about to say, "we can use phonics to make words and sentences."

"B, A, Bay." Lock grinned, using Robert's example from the teachings of *The Three Stooges*.

Willa smiled, but she let him know there was more to it. "*Biggy Bi Bo Bu* may mean something in one language, but have different meaning in another. Pronouncing the sounds isn't helpful unless you can reference a meaning. Like the Rosetta Stone, we've isolated identical content in three languages. We can break the code."

By the time both Lock and Willa were on the same page, they arrived at the river-site Sam chose to build the schoolhouse. They paused, silent from admiration of the view, then they waded upstream until finding a flat sitting-rock rising above the cold water.

The stone, in the center of the stream, nestled under fans of clustered Queen Palms. As they sat, with feet dangling in the water, feathery, breeze-blown branches made an optical illusion on the surface. Dappled, dancing sparkles, gave the impression of flashing lights jitterbugging upstream against the current.

Long moments of kicking water and enjoying the caress of palm-fanned air passed before Lock broke the spell by asking, "Shori can understand some content on the *quipus*?"

"Phonetically, yes. Any *quipucamayac* from Shori's tribe could sound B, A, Bay. They would need to know the other two languages to translate the sounds into words."

Willa turned her face toward the palms above her and exhaled like a sprinter in the blocks, clearing her lungs for a fresh batch of air. "There is a dedication on each *quipu* that is the key for turning *Biggy Bi Bo Bu* into words the reader understands.

"Each *quipu* has six lines of identical dedication, but each line is split into three different languages. Like your four-part map, they must be aligned properly for an ordered reading of the whole. Just as Dorothy said, 'They belong together.' The Naples and Caral *Quipu* have a seventh line in the dedication, not represented on the beast."

Lock halted Willa's lessons. "I'm impressed," he said. "Can you just tell me what they say?"

Willa's body tensed. "I'm going to give you all seven lines of the dedication. Brace yourself."

"Okay, Willa. Consider me braced."

Pachacamac, Our pact is an eternal chain.
Inevitable is reversible.
We have obtained the light.
We hold the star map.
Pachacamac, we preserve the secrets of earth and time in your
    silver book.
Be appeased, Oh Lord. Return and be appeased.

"Marduk!" Lock stiffened, then slid off the rock, up to his waist in cold water. "How many more names can old Baal Zebub claim?"

"As many names as links in a chain, is my guess." Willa slid into the water and embraced Lock. "If Pachacamac is Marduk, we need to talk about something. I believe Alayat wrote the dedication, and he holds the silver book. What could Alayat do with the secrets of earth and time."

"Alayat." Lock squeezed Willa hard when he understood. "I let him get away."

"There's more to hear, John. Parts only Dorothy can read. Well, maybe only Dorothy and the angels. The second language on the *quipus* is in the tongue of The Adam."

Lock closed his eyes and submerged under water, staying down for long seconds. When he re-emerged, he had a question. "Dorothy said there was an impossible language?"

"Yes, we're stumped." Willa looked dejected. "It's not a part of the three languages. There's just a smattering of it on the *quipus*, but it has to be important."

Lock dipped under the surface again but popped up quickly, next to Willa. She shivered and stepped into him, "It's almost lunch time. Let's head back. I'll tell you more on the way. Are you any good with numbers?"

"I know a guy," Lock slapped water and clenched his jaw. "If you have number problems, find Otis Beckley. He's among the missing, with Robert McKinney and Baal Alayat."

41

O TIS STRETCHED, AND RAN HIS HANDS over the pocket of his shirt. "You don't know where I can find myself a glow-in-the-dark pocket protector, do you? I would be grateful. I need to project that image of being a 'numbers guy'."

Doctor Milton raised himself from his chair slowly and shook the tingle out of his sleeping foot. "Can't find those anymore, but I have something in my office I want to get. It could take a while. Would you like more coffee?"

"How about something cold? That is, if you could loan me some cash for the vending machines." Otis smiled mischievously. "I don't know my credit score, but I'm good for it."

"I'll have to stop by the ETM and get you a money card. By the way, how are you going to get around without ID and plastic?"

"I have options. As soon as I leave here, I'm going to pick up my ride in Nevada. Trust me, I'm good as gold."

"Okay Mr. Beckley. You have connections. What are you drinking?"

"Do they have root beer?"

"Dr. Milton hesitated before answering. "Do you want it with or without *Brain Slap?*"

Otis shook his head. "Make it water," he said.

On the way out the door, Dr. Milton stopped, as if suddenly struck by a thought. "Otis," he said. "Don't disappear on me. I have something you'll want to see."

"I promise." Otis ducked into the restroom, muttering about disco pants and glowing shoes.

42

PANAMA
APRIL 23, 2007

W ILLA STOOD AT THE DOORWAY to the guest house watching Dorothy and Huana walk down the path to the looms. "I wish she would show us her new project," she said to Lock. "She's given up her morning fishing routine to work on it. The girl is a riddle."

Lock stacked Dorothy's empty dishes onto his plate and poured the last half-cup of breakfast coffee. "After all the *quipu* talk yesterday, I'm full to the top with riddles."

"Recap what you remember. I'll do the dishes." Willa took the banana peels from the table and added them to the compost bag. "And, when you go to the warehouse with Dorothy, don't forget to take out the compost."

"I'm not going to the warehouse with Dorothy. I'm taking the dinghy back, then, after lunch, I'm joining Dorothy in a round of the hiding game. She's going to hide on the tower, and I'm going to find her." Lock pushed the dishes he stacked toward Willa's plate and leaned backward in his chair. "I hope."

"You hope? For what?" Willa paused from gathering dishes and tilted her head.

"I hope I find her."

"Oh, that should be easy. She's going to be on the tower." Willa laughed at her joke, then returned to *quipus*. "Go ahead, I'm listening. I want to hear your recap."

"Before that ..." Lock sipped his coffee. The worry lines surfaced on his face. "I have sniggling issues about what we discussed yesterday."

Willa took the plates from the table to the sink. "I know what you're thinking, John. You're wondering how much the X-Club has learned from the *quipus*."

Lock gathered the milk and syrup from the table and stood. "More specifically, about New York. Waldo and the Jesuit told you things in New York about how the Caral government worked. Did they pick that up from the *quipus*? Somewhere else?"

Willa plopped the plates down on the sink counter, then opened the cabinet door for Lock to put away the syrup. "I don't know. They're always so far ahead, but let's not ponder which came first, an old egg or a young chicken. Without Dorothy and the idol, I don't see how they translate more than a few disconnected words."

Lock stared through the doorway, toward the path to his downed 'copter. "I need to figure out a safer place for the beast."

"Dorothy says she's almost done cataloging the symbols," Willa picked up the soap bottle and squeezed. "Let her do her work, then we can figure out how to get the idol back on the 'copter when it's ready to fly."

Lock refocused his thoughts on the *quipus* and began to recap. "The knots tell a story about two brother-gods. Together, they emerge from caves near Aymara, or as it's known today, Lake Titicaca. They announce they represent their lord, Pachacamac, who claims he created the sun, but is invisible, flies away, or turns himself into a stone. Right so far?"

Willa faced the sink and turned on the water. "The legends give all three options. The *quipu* says he flew off."

"Okay, let's stick with what's on the *quipus*. No legend evolutions or name changes. There are two brother-gods.

Varicocha takes credit for creating man from clay after his brother, Inti, creates the earth. Varicocha is the god who built Caral, correct?"

"Not exactly, John. He teaches men how to build it."

"The people who built it. They rule the Andes desert for thousands of years by creating an elite class who control education, information, resources, a mystery mix of psychotropic drugs, and a system of strategic manipulation. Their priest class governs for the elite, performs ceremonies, and has the power to make men go mad. Each New Year, they ask for Pachacamac to return, and 'be appeased'. Close enough?"

"Almost. Strategic manipulation isn't mentioned on the *quipu*, John. It's a goal of the X-Club."

Lock swirled the last of the coffee in his cup and watched the grounds settle before going on. "Not trying to put old eggs before young chickens again, but how does it turn out that Huxley's city and Caral are so similar?"

"Great minds think alike? I don't know."

"Willa," Lock wrung his hands together, "I have knots in my stomach. We need to ask Huana about the timing of her sister's personality change and the arrival of Waldo. I don't think he's here to passively observe anything."

"I believe you're right, John. He is a director in the Soma project."

"One more reason to get rid of Waldo." Lock looked at the floor when the words came out of his mouth. "I want you to know, I'll go all the way with him if I have to."

Willa squeezed her eyes tight and tensed, but she ignored the fatal suggestion in the comment. "Soma isn't the only issue," she said. "There's the Silver Book, the star map, the little balls that aren't toys, and the secrets of earth and time."

"Star maps, three-layered balls, and the secrets of earth and time." Lock's head bobbed up and down, as if voting in the affirmative. "Uh-Huh, I'll get right on it."

Willa lowered her eyes, recognizing Lock was overwhelmed, then changed the subject when she noticed the sun touch the corner of the table. "Look," she said, "the sun's begun its mid-morning routine of slipping through the window and creeping across the table." She grabbed a wet cloth and wiped crumbs into her hand, then tossed them in the trash. "Crumbs are like vampires," she said. "Have to put 'em in their coffins when the sun comes up."

"You're getting weirder every day. I love you." Lock flicked a missed crumb with his finger and looked into Willa's surprised face. "It just slipped out," he said. "I meant to ask you something else."

Willa crossed to the other side of the table and put her hands on both sides of Lock's face. "I'm a sucker for tender words. Ask me anything."

"I need to get the *Wally K* back to the north dock. I'll row, you tell me about *quipus*, then we'll stop by the river and take a dip before lunch."

Willa kissed him on the forehead. "So much for tender moments, eh? You row, I'll go."

43

THE *WALLY K* GLIDED SMOOTHLY with each stroke of the oars, but the chopping slap of the waves against wood distracted Lock from his concentration on what Willa was telling him.

When they beached at the helicopter port, Lock asked for a break. "I want to cut a pineapple for lunch, take a dip, then play the hiding game with Dorothy. I'm not able to follow you right now. Three-layered balls for modeling the purified direction of energy, spiritual resonance, and vibration stabilization is over my head on my best day. I'll give it another shot later."

Willa held the boat steady while Lock unhooked the oars and jumped out. "I'm not trying to explain the balls. I'm as lost as you are. Time is racing by. We have seven days until the ceremony. Sam and Shori can return at any time. We're missing a door and a rotor assembly. Dorothy wants to stay, but we can't leave her here if we make a mess of things. We have one week. A sweet pineapple, a cool dip, and some carefully chosen words, released intentionally, might help."

"Carefully chosen words?"

"Yes, not words that slip out." Willa flashed a steak knife in front of Lock's face and smiled. "I love you too, John, Let's go behead a pineapple and take a skinny-dip. I left a note for Dorothy. There's egg salad in the fridge. We can be a little late."

44

R ETURNING TO THE GUEST HOUSE with a river-chilled pineapple,
Lock and Willa didn't expect to find Huana in the kitchen, but
there she was.

"Hi, dudes," Huana greeted them cheerfully. "I have a message
from Dorothy."

Willa pulled up a chair next to Huana and waited for her to
swallow the giant bite of egg salad sandwich before prompting
her. "What is the message, dear?"

Huana reached for her water. "I sounded out some of it." She
tilted her head and pursed her lips together. "I know some of the
big words, because Dorothy taught me *t-i-o-n* spells 'shun' at the
end of a word."

Willa answered patiently, "Dorothy gave you something for
us to read?"

"Yes. She wrote it on paper. *I found the dewer ... yada yada ...
cut the ... something something ... take back graduation papers.* I'm
getting better, but she wrote it in cursive."

Lock walked toward Huana and didn't use his patient voice. "Where is the message, Huana?"

Huana eyed Lock while she drank her water down in one long gulp, followed by a satisfied, "Aah, that was good." She made Lock wait under her stare a little longer before saying, "So like, chill, dude, I have it in my pocket."

Willa took control, telling Lock, "John, don't you have to go meet Dorothy at the tower? After Huana gives us the message, you'll need to hurry. Us girls will stay here and have a little talk." She pulled her chair closer to Huana and asked, "Dorothy is waiting for Mr. Lockjaw at the tower, isn't she?"

"Yes."

"Would you stay and talk with me after we read the message?"

Huana reached into her pocket and pulled out a folded sheet of paper and turned her stare on Willa. Handing her Dorothy's message, she asked suspiciously, "Talk about what?"

Without losing eye contact with the young girl, Willa handed the folded message to Lock and offered Huana some assurance. "I study how people live in groups and find ways to be happy together. Can you teach me about the people on the island? I want to hear about your sister."

Lock paused from unfolding the message when he recognized a change in Huana's *so-what* facial facade. Her stare stayed frozen in place, but a visible cloudiness crossed her face like passing shade. Huana fought to hold on to her attitude, but her stare soon collapsed into a lip-quivering, head-down retreat.

Willa wrapped her arms around her and said, "I know people aren't happy when they worry about their families. That's why I need your help. You have passion and spirit — like Dorothy. Can you tell me when the adults lost their spirit?"

Lock caught Willa's attention with a quizzical look and a prolonged shoulder shrug, palms up.

Willa nodded to the note and answered Lock's silent question. "I guess my curiosity is back on the front burner."

Turning his back to the girls, Lock opened the note and walked to the porch, reading it to himself as he went.

Dear Mr. and Mrs. Willa and Lockjaw,

Greetings. Miss manners likes me to write a casual correspondence letter, so I will practice now.

I heard men say they were going to cut down the palmettos by your helicopter, so I went to the warehouse to get a shovel for digging a hole. I put a secret into the hole. Huana helped me push it in, but I didn't tell her what it was.

When I went to the warehouse to return the shovel, I did something impulsive and bad. I snooped. I hope you don't take back my graduation papers.

I heard a noise and it made me think. When I climb the tower behind the warehouse, I can see a noisy box on the window. So now I am wondering. Why is there a box on the window in the back of the warehouse if there is no window inside the warehouse?

I found a secret room and touched a lot of things I don't know about. Some of those things have books to teach me, so if I can snoop again, I will know which knobs and switches, and bottles to touch.

The door for your helicopter is in the secret room. I will show you when you come play the hiding game.

Regards,

Your best friend, Dorothy.

P.S. Please tell Huana that an air conditioner is a storehouse of the snows at the top and bottom of the world. It makes the currents in the big water wag like serpent tails. I know this from reading 'The Secrets of Enoch', the Ethiopic translation. Huana thinks an air conditioner is a box on a window. I try to teach her better.

XOXOXO (Optional)

45

L OCK JOGGED TO THE WAREHOUSE and looked for Dorothy. Once again, she and the tower were invisible. "You win," he shouted into the vines. "Come down, we need to talk."

"Don't let your mind trick you, Mr. Lockjaw. A tower isn't always high high. I'm down here." Dorothy waved her arm and Lock spotted the movement, just three feet above the rooftop.

The arm waving stopped suddenly, and Dorothy pointed upward, to a spot over Lock's head, "Can you see it? Mr. Sam is back."

Before he saw it, he heard it. The sound of an incoming helicopter grew louder, then it flashed over the warehouse clearing, headed to the heliport.

Lock, torn between exploring a secret room and hurrying to meet Sam, made an impulsive choice. "Show me the room," he shouted.

After Dorothy demonstrated the trick to gain entry, they stood in the open doorway, taking inventory of what was around them.

Attached to the back wall, where the window air conditioning unit hummed, a deep, nearly empty shelf spread the length of the room.

One item on the shelf stood out: a dorm-room-style refrigerator.

Between the refrigerator and the air conditioner, a pile of books sat under a movie poster featuring the smiling Griswold family. The Griswolds, waving to the camera under the logo of the fictitious *Wally World,* hung to the right of the air conditioner.

Taking the rest of the wall space between appliances was another poster. Through the familiar banner of *Barnum and Bailey Circus,* a clown in a hot pink wig, sporting a demented smile, appears to burst through the page, offering a bouquet of squirting flowers.

Dorothy waved her arm slowly toward the right side of the room, like a real estate agent showing features in a house. "Against the wall," she said, "a small cot, the bedding unmade. The pillow still retains the dent of the last head to rest there."

Waving her left arm toward the other side of the room, she pointed to a beige curtain, draped from ceiling to floor, and from wall to wall.

"Just like Oz," she said. "There's not a man behind the curtain, but there are machines with knobs and buttons. One of them has a looking screen like Willa's computer. Also, there is a tall stool and a door for your bird."

Lock opened the refrigerator and rummaged through the shelves. Dozens of four-ounce medical vials, seals broken, filled with clear liquids, shared space with a six-pack of drinking water in plastic bottles. While moving the bottles around to search the back of the shelves, Lock noticed he recognized only a few of the chemical names on the bottle. "Strychnine, acetaminophen, sodium amytal, and digitalis," he said aloud. "Welcome to Wally's world."

Dorothy nervously watched Lock examine the refrigerator contents, her shoulders hunched, hands twisted under her chin, and one finger pulling at her bottom lip. "Don't handle any of the bottles in there," she said. "You can read about what's in them in the red book on the shelf. It's called *The Physicians Desk Reference.*"

Lock picked up the thick red *PDR*, then set it back in place after reading the title. "How much time have you spent in here?" he asked, while moving over to the curtain.

"Just one morning. I sorry."

When Lock pushed the curtains open, he saw the reason for the tower. "A ham radio," he said, then quickly avoided questions by telling Dorothy, "It has nothing to do with pigs." He held up the manual. "If we learn this book and use that radio, we can talk to the world."

Behind him, Lock heard a sound come out of Dorothy he didn't recognize, part moan and part rapturous gasp. When he turned to see her, he knew by her open-mouth, wide-eyed stare at the radio that Dorothy was smitten. "Don't touch anything," he said, "until we read the manual and learn how to use it."

Dorothy responded to Lock's instructions with a question. "You mean the whole world?"

Lock realized he needed to rush to the heliport, so he gave Dorothy instructions. "I mean don't touch it. Don't touch anything. I have to meet Sam. You need to put the room back, just the way you found it, then go tell Willa Sam is back. Tell her to wait for me."

Lock bolted through the door, then slid to a stop. "Don't tell anyone but Willa about the secret room."

Off he went to greet Sam.

The sound of the outside door of the warehouse slamming shut jarred Dorothy loose from her trance. "The whole world," she whispered, while reaching for the manual. She read the words on the cover and introduced herself. "Hello, Mr. *Model C-437A Digital Ham Radio Operators Manual.* My name is Dorothy. I have to run and tell Willa something, but I'll be back to let you teach me to talk to the whole world."

46

FIFTEEN MINUTES AFTER DOROTHY ARRIVED at the guesthouse with Lock's messages, a sudden rumbling sound, very much like thunder, caught the attention of the three girls sitting at the kitchen table.

"Odd," Willa remarked, while looking out the window at the sky. "This is the first day, since we've been here, where the sky is completely cloudless."

"It's too early for the rain," Huana added.

"My ears say the noise wasn't thunder from Heaven." Dorothy walked to the porch and sniffed the air. "I think we all need to play the hiding game."

"It had to be thunder," Willa gripped the table and looked at Dorothy, "It has to be. I think we all have the heebee jeebees."

"What are we scared of?' Huana asked.

"We're scared of heebee jeebees," Dorothy answered, "because we don't know what they are, and they make loud noises."

187

Willa calmed herself after hearing Dorothy's description and chuckled. "It's probably nothing. You girls should go ahead with your afternoon routine. I'll wait here for John."

*   *   *

Dorothy and Huana left the guesthouse in silence. When Dorothy didn't take the path to the looms, Huana didn't question her, she followed. The silent walk ended at the warehouse.

"I don't want to scare Willa," Dorothy said, when they stopped walking. "It's been a long time since I've heard the boom of explosions. I need to find Sam and Mr. Lockjaw, and I want you to play the hiding game."

"I'm not hiding for fun, am I?" Huana nodded her head in recognition of Dorothy's serious expression. "Fist bump, dude. Tell me, what's the deal."

"Explosions mean people are killing people. On purpose. The last time I heard explosions, the Savant were burned down to their bones. Maybe the Americans are coming to kill us."

"Maybe the Peru men?" Huana's eyes widened.

"Maybe the Nazis, or the Muslims, or the Huns, or the Contras, or ..." Dorothy quit checking down her list of possible blood-spillers and admitted she didn't know who the enemy might be. "Maybe somebody I haven't read about. Whoever it is, we need an army."

"Oh." Huana sat cross-legged, in the path and groaned. "I'm not sure how to find an army."

"George Patton knows how to make an army," Dorothy said with confidence. "He said, to make an army, you gather fluff and work it into a string. Then you pull the string uphill, because you can't push a string uphill. He meant people, not fluff. I try to be clear."

"I'm ready to be fluffed and pulled uphill," Huana declared without hesitation.

Dorothy put her hands up to her chin in the prayer position and walked a circle in the path. At the end of her circle, she said, "I've got it. Mr. Sam needs to tell everybody we're at war, then Mr.

Lockjaw can fluff everybody into string, just like he fluffed the Montagnard tribe."

Huana shot an angry glance at Dorothy, "No, hell no. Didn't the Montagnard lose their land? He shot his own Grampy. I want to beat these snakes into ant food and get my tribe back. We should talk to Willa. She knows who the enemy is, and his name is Mr. Wally."

"We need good intelligence." Dorothy led Huana into the warehouse and opened the door to the secret room. "This is Wally's world. We can find intelligence here."

"We're not stupid, Dorothy." Huana stepped into the room and sat on the cot. "We just don't know what we're doing."

"In wartime, intelligence isn't knowing what we know. Intelligence is knowing what the enemy knows. If we know what the enemy knows, we can make him not know what we know he knows and make him think he knows enough to make a bad plan." Dorothy peeked behind the curtain. "First we look around for what he knows. I try to be clear."

Huana scratched her face, then rubbed her wrinkled brow. "Intelligence makes you smart, but you get intelligence from your enemy and it makes him stupid. I think it sounds like a Bruja. They feed a person *ayahuasca*, then they steal positive vibrations when the head spirit comes. Is that our plan?"

Dorothy hopped onto the tall stool behind the curtain and opened the manual for the ham radio. "First we gather, then we think, then we make a plan. Look around the room for clues about Mr. Wally, but don't touch the bottles in the refrigerator. They're dangerous."

Huana opened the refrigerator door and asked, "Is the water dangerous?"

"It's okay if the seal isn't broken." Before Dorothy could tell Huana to leave the bottled water alone, she heard the snap of the plastic seal. Hopping back down off the stool, she peeked through the curtains and saw Huana draining the bottle.

"I have a mission for you," Dorothy said, after watching Huana finish the water in one long gulp. "Run to the refrigerator at the guest house and get a new six-pack of water. We need to make it look like we were never here."

Huana ran out of the room. Dorothy waited for the slam of the warehouse door, then she went to the fridge and removed a bottle of water for herself. "Kids," she mumbled, then hopped back onto the stool and, once again, opened the manual.

Before Huana reached the guest house, Dorothy identified all the buttons, switches, and knobs on the radio. One by one, she learned their functions. After reading the troubleshooting chapter, she noticed a familiar symbol and turned, as the book suggested, to the index.

"Mushka, Sheeshka Mushka!" she shouted, noticing the schematic diagram of the radio. The symbols in the schematic, cross-referenced to their functions, held Dorothy's rapt attention. "Impossible language, my aching booty! Talk to me, Mr. Index."

By the time Huana returned, sheets of paper with Dorothy's scribbling were scattered around the counter. Like a horse racing bettor trying to figure out trifecta combinations, symbols on the paper were sorted in combinations of three, then either crossed out or given a number for grouping. The process so engrossed Dorothy she became absorbed into the zone of the mind where chunks of time pass without notice. The slam of the warehouse door jerked her out of her zone and into a cleaning frenzy.

Dorothy tried to gather her papers, until the sound of the door to the secret room being unlocked ended her manic scrambling. She held her breath and peeked through the curtain, wincing at the disarray in the room. When she saw it was Huana, she returned to gathering papers.

In the tunnel vision of her excitement over the symbols, Dorothy didn't immediately recognize Huana's condition. "I have learned to talk to the world, and I'm learning to make a machine to talk to the world." she crowed. "I have good news for Willa."

Dorothy didn't stop her chatter when Huana didn't respond. "I want you to do something for me," she said. "I want you to hide all the little squares I made on the looms, then hide yourself."

Huana still didn't respond, but Dorothy sorted her papers and pushed through the curtain, holding the stack in front of her. "Take the sheet on top and follow the ..."

After noticing Huana, curled up on the cot in the fetal position, Dorothy put her papers on the long shelf and sat next to her, stroking her hair. "Huana?"

The moment Huana felt the touch, she wailed into the pillow. "We're all going to die."

47

"I'M RUNNING OUT OF INSIDE INFORMATION, DOC." Otis's voice was soft and flat. "I'm going to leave you wanting more details."

"Why is that?" Dr. Milton asked, raising his eyes at the somber tone.

Otis fidgeted with the rolled-up cuffs on his shirt before answering. "I can tell you what happens up to a point. I need to tell it cold — like numbers. I don't know how anything in Panama ends, but what I do know ... cold, like numbers."

Dr. Milton sighed and loosened his tie. "In my experience, the devil isn't in the drama. The drama is genuflection, a mask of symptoms, hiding the disease. I'm okay with 'cold, like numbers'. "What is the one, two, three of it?"

48

W HEN HUANA REACHED THE GUESTHOUSE, Willa was at the kitchen table, typing at the computer. The news that Sam and Shori were back on the island was welcomed with a sigh of relief. "Good," she told Huana, "now we can talk to Sam about Mr. Wally. Will you stay with me while we wait for John?"

Huana declined. She had little woven squares to hide, so she gave Willa a hug and headed for the door.

The sound of laughing made her stop walking. It made Willa stand abruptly, knocking her chair over as she backed away from the table. She recognized the stilted tone of the laugh: the guffaw of a demented clown.

"Huana, hide in the closet," Willa barked abruptly. "Just do it. The closet, now."

"Sam and Shori are coming here." Huana pointed through the doorway. "Mr. Wally is walking up the path from the boat dock."

"Huana!" Willa hissed her words. "The closet. Now."

That's how it happened. That's how Huana lost innocence through her ears and eyes. The words and sounds were amplified in the darkness of the closet. Glimpses through a keyhole, framed scenes of horror. Huana witnessed a perfect recipe for nightmares.

"There's old Willa girl," Sam belted as he walked through the door. "How's things?" His tone, cheerful as usual.

"Things are going swimmingly," Willa replied in a voice matching Sam's sunny greeting. "Did you see John? He left to meet you at the heliport."

Even Shori sounded pleasantly sunny. "Yes, we saw John. It was great."

"We gave him a new helicopter," Sam interjected. "A thank-you for his generous donations to our sanctuary project. He's already taken the new bird out for a test drive."

"I can't wait to hear all about it." Huana heard Willa's footsteps in the kitchen. "I need to make coffee. Will you stay and have a cup? When is John coming back?"

"John? Did I give you the impression John would be back? You didn't hear him go boom?" Chuckles from Shori followed Sam's comment.

Huana held her breath. A long, strained silence ended with the sound of a coffee pot shattering on the kitchen floor.

Shori cackled and shouted too loudly, "I pressed a button and made it go boom."

Huana heard the wail rise in Willa's throat, and flinched when it exploded out of her mouth in a growl. The noises that followed — loud sounds of chaos and struggle — were brief. At one point, Shori screamed a warning, "She's going for the steak knives again!"

The sounds of battle ended with a dull thump of something heavy falling to the floor, followed by a sudden hush.

Everything went so suddenly still, Huana could hear the creaking stairs and footsteps on the porch, followed by the voice of Waldo Kurtwood. "Was it the dart, or did she faint?"

Sam reached down and flicked a dart protruding from Willa's neck. "She's dying. Let's just get her into a body bag and move her."

"Oh, no," Shori chimed, "I want to watch the lights go out."

The cheerfulness in Shori's voice curdled the stomach of the terrified Huana. She pulled herself into a ball and shivered at the happy sounding cruelty of cats playing with a dying mouse.

Waldo pushed her terror level a little higher with his vote on how to handle the helpless Willa. "We can keep her alive until the curare wears off, or maybe just until I've had some fun with her. She misses me. Look, you can see the excitement in her eyes."

Hearing that Willa was still alive jolted Huana. She untangled herself and sat upright, leaning to get a glimpse through the keyhole. She saw Wally, dangling a long plastic bag over his shoulder, straddling Willa's prone figure. "How come you quit taking my calls, sweety?"

"Keep your sick self under wraps," Sam said. "We have a lot to get done."

Shori cooed her vote, "Just a little fun?"

"Look at those shiny eyes, Sam." Wally wasn't giving up on his party plans. "Is it excitement or fear?"

Wally's argument ended at the abrupt crack of a pistol, followed by two voices in tandem. "Aww ... What the hell?"

"Fun with curare is over," Sam said.

After Huana watched Sam step forward and fire a round into Willa's face, she jerked her eye away from the keyhole and wet herself, the guzzled water of her morning soaking her sweatpants. Sam ended the torture of a wide-awake mind, taunted in a paralyzed body, but Huana was certain, Willa Vernon, as well as John Lockjaw Smith, were dead. Their adventures in the short life, over.

Sam's voice confirmed it. "Shori, grab a trash bag and put it under her head."

A song from Wally made the whole thing unbearably sickening. "Goodbye cruel world. You're off to join the circus."

"Wally!" Sam responded forcefully, "Don't stand and gawk. Get her in the bag." It was clear, Sam, the great savior of Huana's tribe, was the leader of this pack.

Huana sat for long moments. Silence, interspersed with grunts and rustling sounds, lasted until the steady buzz of a long zipper being closed announced a chore completed.

Shivering from an overdose of fear, Huana no longer tried to look through the keyhole, she sat and listened while the three murderers confirmed deadly plans.

"Wally, did you bring the Jonestown mix? I want it fast acting, not your funny chicken-dance-'til-you-die crap. Just dead, nothing else."

"Got ya boss." Waldo sounded resigned to the plan. "I'll do a remix."

"Shori." Sam barked her name. "I'm going to check out the progress at the banyan tree. Tell everyone to bring the children to the ceremony this month, and get me some boys to drag this bag to the boat."

"And tell that girl, Caspi, to come to the guesthouse," Wally added. "I've had a stressful day."

"When we find Dorothy, I want to drown her," Shori offered. I've wanted to drown her since I met her." Shori's voice was deadpan, emotionless, determined.

Sam's frustrated voice answered, "Dammit, Shori. Boogers under the table."

The sound of kitchen chairs scooted back and forth across the floor filled the closet until Sam issued a calm command.

"All clear."

He followed his prompt with a request for Waldo.

"When this is over, I want you to give Shori a new compliance-check trigger. This booger thing isn't funny anymore."

Wally responded by reminding Sam of the boundaries between them. "My department, my call. I'll handle the mind-engineering, you tell me how you want to handle Dorothy."

"Take her alive. If she won't let us, put her on ice immediately." Sam spoke forcefully. "Ice is not our best option. We'll get better DNA if we take her alive. Do you understand me Shori?"

"Take the little *bruja* alive." The tone of disappointment in Shori's voice lilted into a mischievous note. "Unless she won't let us."

Footsteps growing softer gave Huana the courage to reach for the door handle and peek through the keyhole again. She opened the door a crack after hearing creaking on the stairs.

*   *   *

"I watched them take their separate paths," Huana recounted to Dorothy. "Dr. Frankenstein, his insane bride, and the mad assistant, Igor. The villagers can't work up enough fear to grab torches and pitchforks. I wet my pants, Caspi is going to be raped, you might be dissected like a frog, and we're all going to die. I have no more intelligence to report."

The two brokenhearted friends rocked back and forth in a joyless embrace. Huana, trembled, and cried dry tears.

Dorothy was stiff, her normally soft eyes transformed into hard slits as they stared at the door. The two of them held on to each other until grief allowed them room to think. When they stepped back from the hug, Dorothy spoke softly. "Have you used up all your courage?"

"I have enough left to die fighting in the war." Huana said plainly, like she had already taken inventory."

"I see. I see," Dorothy repeated. "We know where Wally, Sam, and Shori are going. Run to the *agllawasi*, then take Caspi to the river. Take the river all the way to the head-spring. I'll meet you there."

Huana hesitated, taking a false step toward the door, then stopped. "I want to know what you're going to do."

"I have muscles like a howler monkey," Dorothy boasted, while making a tiny fist. "I have eyes like a jaguar, and the mind of a Savant. First, I will talk to the world and tell them about children and families in danger. After I talk to the world, I'm sending some crazy people to judgment."

"I like your plan," Huana said. Then she lingered a moment before racing off. "Fist pump, Dude. I'll see you at the spring."

Dorothy waited for the slam of the warehouse door, then walked across the room and straight through the curtains to the ham radio. Without referring to the manual, she flipped switches and adjusted dials, ready to send out her call for help to the whole world.

Dorothy paused with the microphone in her hand and prayed. When she finished her prayer, she pressed a button and spoke. "*Neela mushka Lo amili. Bo amalee jhova. Sheeshka asant zn.*" An appeal to the angels, in the original of languages, went out into the ethers.

One angel in particular responded quickly. Kae'Lairy slammed our windows in the box shut and blasted a path back to earth, setting down on an island off of Panama, where he showed his respect for our free will by being of no help at all.

49

O TIS ROLLED HIS BIG BLUE MARBLE back and forth in his hands and snorted as if he'd been assaulted with a sudden odor.

"Have you ever been disgusted with God? I mean, you know, the old question. Why does God allow bad things to happen?"

Dr. Milton raised his eyelids and looked up at Otis, pausing long enough to make him stop fidgeting with the ball and make eye contact. "Not since I realized I knew how to ride my bicycle," he said, after their eyes locked.

Otis shook his head like he was erasing an image on an Etch-A-Sketch and asked, "You were answering my question?"

"I learned how to ride a bike the traditional way," Dr. Milton answered patiently. "My father held onto the seat, running alongside me, until he knew I was in control. The thing is, I didn't know I was in control. When I sensed he wasn't holding me, I panicked. A rose bush, a curb, our cat loomed in front of me. There was wide-open space as well, but I didn't guide myself into the open. I dove off the bike, skinning my knees, scraping my hands, angry at my father for the dirty trick. I didn't trust him until I realized what happened. Within the hour, I was a free man with the wind in my face, pedaling the tricky turns around my yard and begging to be allowed to ride in the street. I can picture my old bicycle routes today, but I can't tell you where my scrapes were. Distrusting God is as temporary to me as distrusting my father for allowing me to realize I had control. Doubting his existence is another matter. When we're done here, I'll show you what I mean."

Dr. Milton leaned in his chair to get a look down the hallway, then turned his attention back to Otis.

"Nurse Station chatter," he said. "New patient coming in. Do we need to discuss this blame-God-for-the-bicycle any further? It's your ride, take the handlebars or jump off. If you can't do either, make an appointment. I'll see you as a patient."

"A little harsh, don't you think, Doc?"

"I'm jealous of the exotic bicycle you've been given to ride. Pedal hard and be thankful, like Dorothy."

"Yeah, Doc, like Dorothy. She pedaled right into a semi."

"Tell me about it."

50

D OROTHY SAT ATOP THE STOOL, listening for angels. During the wait, she drifted to thoughts of Lock and Willa, picturing the three of them in Eden, flying over the Amazon, sitting at meals in the guest house, laughing and screaming with the children on movie night.

She clenched at the sudden memory of Sam and Shori walking through the storm after the day of the stinky-hut fiasco. She shuddered after questioning her responsibility for the mass murder being planned for Huana and her tribe.

"I sorry!" Dorothy screamed the words aloud and jumped off her stool, tearing the curtains from the ceiling, kicking the stool over, then picking it up and smashing it into the wall. "You better come fast," she screamed at the ceiling. "I'm not going to wait."

When no answer came to her ultimatum, Dorothy tore the bedding off the cot and threw them around the room. "I don't care if you know I was here," she said to the clown on the poster. "I'm coming to let you know."

Dorothy froze in her one-way stare-down that ended when the words she spoke came back to her in a new context. There were things they shouldn't know. Willa had video on her computer she didn't want anyone to see. She was embarrassed for having snooped and seen them.

The results of all those nights when she worked with Willa to decipher the *quipus* were recorded on Willa's teaching machine. It was important to keep the results secret.

Dorothy flew through the warehouse in a dead run toward the guesthouse, taking the path to the boat dock. She arrived at the dock in time to see two men unloading the *Wally K.*

One of the men jumped into the boat and threw two duffel bags, a gym bag, and a suitcase into a pile on the dock, setting them next to a long, lumpy plastic bag lying next to the pylon.

When the boat was unloaded, the man on shore threw a duffel bag over his shoulder and walked toward the guesthouse. The man in the boat rolled the big plastic bag into the boat with him. The heavy bag thudded onto the wooden seats, rocking the boat enough to make waves.

Dorothy hyperventilated in rhythm with the lapping waves as they hit the shore. She bit her hand to keep from crying out when the man stepped on the bag to hop onto the dock. She knew from what Huana told her, Willa was in the bag.

The man picked up the gym bag and the suitcase, then followed down the path to the guesthouse. When he cleared the big fern, Dorothy scrambled to the dock, hopped into the boat and unzipped the lumpy bag.

Willa's face, bloodied, stared past Dorothy with clouded eyes. Dorothy closed her friend's lids gently, brushed her cheek and said goodbye. "I sorry," she said softly. "Tell Mr. Lockjaw I will see both of you in Heaven. Let Asitr know I saw the world. He was right not to take me with him. I'm a disaster."

Dorothy zipped Willa back up and pulled herself onto the dock, examining the remaining duffel bag with her hands before opening it. "You don't feel like Huana," she said. "You feel like a place for me to hide."

The first thing Dorothy noticed when she opened the duffel bag was the bright colors inside. She reached in and pulled out a lime green wig. Next she retrieved two giant shoes with sequined polka dots and bright yellow stars. A bag full of colorful noses followed.

"Now there is room for me," she said to the pile, then kicked everything into the water and climbed into the bag, holding the opening closed with her hands.

She didn't wait long. She heard footsteps and felt the change in gravity as the bag was hoisted over a shoulder. The bumpy walk to the guesthouse made her tighten her grip. After arriving, her carrier dropped her to the ground, then dragged her up the steps. Each creaking step struck into her bones as she ascended to the porch. Friction from being dragged across the wooden floor burned her skin through the canvas, but she held onto her grip like the warehouse traps held tight to their prey.

"Put it with the other bag," Waldo's voice sent an angry shiver through Dorothy. Once again, she felt the friction of being dragged, the gravity sensation of being tossed, the jolt of impact, then the sound of a door being shut.

For the first time since being lifted over a shoulder, Dorothy allowed herself a long exhale. The inhale brought in a sour odor. It was the smell of Huana's urine. Dorothy knew where she was.

Inside the bag she smiled, then let go of her grip. Silent as a snake, she slowly pulled herself out of the bag and put an eye to the keyhole.

Waldo wasn't in her field of vision, but she heard his footsteps walking away from the closet. She heard the popping of the latches on his suitcase, the sound of cheerful humming, and, again, his footsteps. This time the steps grew louder as he walked into her vision and stopped to sit at the kitchen table.

After nestling into his chair, he pulled Willa's laptop across the table and turned it around to face the screen. "HuHaw!" he exploded as Dorothy saw the screen light up. "Our old Caral project," he laughed. "X-Club property. I should burn your feet with cigarettes."

Waldo began to mumble to himself as he perused her files until he clicked on the video file from New York titled *Asitr's Nugget.* "HuHaw!" He exploded again, after fast forwarding to the second phone call. "You kept a souvenir."

Dorothy watched him scoot back and forth in his chair, punctuating his continual moaning with the occasional expression, "Take it like a man!"

When he stood up from the table, he planted his feet and began thrusting his hips and howling like a wolf. Suddenly, in celebration, he began singing, perverting the words to the *Bonzo Dog Band* parody:

Looking like a muscle man, I crawled out of the swamp.
Slimy wild, my honey child.
I done your brain in.
Yeah, yeah, I done your brain in. Right in.
And you just can't handle it.
Whoopty boogity whoa! I done your brain in.

It was too much for Dorothy.

Waldo spun around at the sound of the closet door slamming into the wall, and stepped backward into the table at the sight of the blur that was Dorothy, flinging herself with a leap into his face.

Her two teeth sunk into his cheek and her thumb found his eye. Waldo fell onto his back, on top of the table. Willa's computer stabbed him painfully in the spine. Kicking at the air, screaming in fear, was ineffectual. Trying to gain control of his tiny attacker proved impossible. The thumb in the eye, the pit bull tenacity of two teeth refusing to stop tearing at his face, together with the new pain of Dorothy's knees stabbing again and again into his kidneys, pushed Waldo's screams louder, more desperate, and significantly more shrill.

"Need help little girl?" The sound of Sam's voice at the doorway didn't stop Waldo's high-pitched scream or the tenacity of the attack. Sam's pistol, fired into the air, was also ineffective.

Dorothy was relentless.

Waldo was a terrified shell of a muscle man from the swamp. His brain, never stable, was done in. Right in. He continued to scream, even after three heavy blows from the butt end of Sam's pistol knocked Dorothy unconscious.

*   *   *

When Dorothy revived, she was propped up on the lounger, confined in a makeshift straight jacket fashioned from Waldo's duffel bag. A padlock secured the opening around Dorothy's neck. Her head stuck out of the top, but her arms and feet were imprisoned inside the canvas. The first thing her eyes focused on was Sam, sitting across from her on the couch.

"Welcome back, Dorothy. I almost had to kill you, and I really don't want to do that." Sam smiled at her, stood, and walked across the room to the lounger. "Now don't bite," he said, as he put his hand on the painful lump at the back of her head. "I can get some ice for that. I have a crateful at the heliport."

"I don't need ice," Dorothy replied. "I need to think better."

"Having trouble thinking straight?" Sam's voice had the tone of concern. "You have a concussion. Mr. Wally has medicine to help you." Sam turned his head toward the kitchen table and laughed. "As soon as Shori can get him patched up."

Dorothy twisted her head toward the kitchen.

Shori was holding a napkin over Waldo's eye and pouring hydrogen peroxide over the jagged rips in his cheek. The foaming peroxide streamed down from his chin and onto his bloody shirt.

"That's a good look for you," Dorothy mocked. "You look like a rabid, one-eyed sloth."

Waldo's one good eye vibrated from side to side in the socket. His pupil was wide open, giving his normally blue eyes the appearance of being coal black. He tried to respond, but a sputtering burst of sounds led to the formulation of only one word. "Smfft, fubble ... bitch." He finished by sweeping his arm across the table, knocking pieces of Willa's computer to the floor and spilling the peroxide.

"When he calms down," Sam said, "he owes you an apology. A good girl like you will forgive him, won't you? What do you say, old girl?"

"Here is what I say, Mr. Pineapple Sam. I am not a good girl. I snoop, then spoil what I learn. Inside, I'm polluted with fast learning and slow knowing."

"What do you know, Dorothy?" Sam knelt down next to the lounger and motioned to Shori, giving her a command. "Have the ice brought to the dock."

Dorothy watched Shori leave the guesthouse, then answered. "Mr. Lockjaw and Willa tried to keep bad things away from me, but I snooped with my ears. Now I know you are the same as Mr. Wally. You want the gifts God gave to my tribe, so you will dissect me like a frog and steal them, because you think I'm a platypus. I have something you can't evolve into and can't create. Too late, you will know you made a mistake."

"What was your mistake, Dorothy? Maybe it would be helpful to learn from your experience."

"I wanted the whole world. Like you. My flaw will curse you, but I will never tell you where the flawless wise ones live, so cut me up and be sorry, like me. You will be true sorry, soon, to make your world into a stinky hut. This is not my curse on you, this is what I know. I try to be clear."

"That was very helpful," Sam said beaming. "Wally, I'm going to check something on Lock's helicopter. Keep her alive until I get back."

Through the doorway, while Sam descended the stairs, Dorothy spotted Huana picking up a hammer in the blacksmith station. "Intelligence, not war," she screamed as loudly as she could.

"Worst t-shirt slogan ever," Waldo snorted.

Huana slid into the shadows. One thumb up indicated she understood.

$$* \qquad * \qquad *$$

With Sam away, and Dorothy in her canvas straitjacket, Waldo regained his composure. He held a wad of paper towels against his face and began opening drawers in the kitchen. Once he found what he was looking for, he showed it to Dorothy.

"You know what this is good for, besides cracking nuts?"

Dorothy didn't answer.

"It's difficult, but if you have strong hands and the good fortune of having a patient with large gaps between teeth, it makes for an excellent dental tool. I'm not expert in the art. My expertise is in arranging synapse trails with chemistry. Dentistry with kitchen utensils is just a hobby. Are you okay with soft foods? Smoothies are good."

Waldo smiled, then recoiled, wincing in pain after stretching the skin around his wounds.

Dorothy tried to look calm, but inside the duffel bag, she was trembling. With her view through the door, she could see a shadow moving toward the guesthouse. From the way the figure inched forward, while swaying in sync with the shadows made by the trees, it was obvious to her it was Huana, putting in practice one of the tricks Dorothy taught her for playing the hiding game.

"I'm not sure I'll eat another meal" she said, "I think my trajectory is no longer intersecting with pleasures in life."

"You underestimate how valuable you are to me." Waldo laid his wad of paper towels on the table and held the nutcracker in both hands. "I have a carrot to offer, along with the stick." Waldo repeatedly snapped the two sides of the nutcracker together, making a series of metallic clanks. The sound brought another wide grin to his face, then he dropped his toy on the floor and reached for the roll of paper towels as blood, again, began seeping from his wounds.

While he folded the towels into a thick mat, Waldo spoke to Dorothy out of one side of his mouth. "Do you know why Sam is in charge here, instead of me?"

Dorothy didn't answer. To distract attention away from Huana's creeping shadow, she began wiggling violently on the lounger. She was on the verge of toppling onto the floor when Waldo walked to her side, his back to the door, and pinned her in place with his free hand.

"I'm trying to save lives, Dorothy. Stop resisting, or this whole tribe will be dead in a few days. You can fight me and they die. Refuse to answer, and you lose your teeth. Or ..."

Waldo pulled his hand away from Dorothy and removed the paper towel, folding it again and putting the dry side onto his wound. "Or," he started again, "we can both get what we want."

Dorothy closed her mouth tight and squeezed her eyes shut, showing Waldo she had no intention of cooperating, but a squeak on the stairs made her eyes pop back open. Huana, she feared, had given herself away.

Waldo was between Dorothy and the door, blocking her view. He turned toward the noise but still, Dorothy was blocked from seeing who was there.

"What!" Waldo shouted.

No answer came.

"Who's there?" he demanded.

"Velas." The answer came in a male voice with flat, indifferent intonation.

Dorothy knew Velas as the man who ran the equipment on movie night.

"What do you want?" Waldo stomped toward the door, impatience in his voice.

"Nothing," Velas said.

"Then what are you doing here?"

"I need to report a failure to Shori."

"Give me the message. I'll tell her when she returns."

"I can't find Caspi."

"Oh," Waldo lowered his voice and shooed Velas away with his hand. "I don't need her anymore. Go."

Waldo spun and hurriedly made his way back to the lounger, stopping on the way to pick the nutcracker off the floor. "We have to hurry," he said. "If you don't tell me what I want to know, I can't save this tribe. If Sam comes back before you tell me, it will be too late." Waldo pushed the nutcracker between Dorothy's lips and pulled the bottom lip down. Turning his swollen eye away from her, he peered into her mouth. "Everything can be fine if you answer one question." He removed the nutcracker to allow her to respond.

"Why should I believe you?"

"Because I believe you know where to find the *Silver Book*." Waldo started to grin but caught himself, squeezing his eye tight as he pushed the towels harder against his facial wound. "The book is more precious than your DNA, more precious than gold, more precious than the X-Club. I want to know its secrets and live forever. For that, you can have this island, and I will bring these spirits back to life."

"Maybe Mr. Sam would like to know what you want." Dorothy's face wrinkled in thought, then she angled her face to try to see past the looming Waldo. "Maybe Mr. Sam would make a deal," she drawled as if thinking aloud. "I think I will live longer than you if he knows what you want to do."

Waldo turned to see the courtyard, then whirled back around, jamming the nutcracker into Dorothy's mouth. "Sam has already decided to let Shori drown you and pack your old, spoiled DNA in ice. Guess what. It's all your fault for telling him the Savant tribe still lives. If he believes he can find them, you become expendable."

"I would never tell him they still live," Dorothy whined, after Waldo removed the nutcracker from her mouth.

"Who were you referring to when you said you would never tell us where the wise ones live?"

"I sorry." Dorothy let her head droop. "Sam will take their DNA, but maybe not find the *Silver Book.*"

Waldo tossed the nutcracker onto the couch and walked to the kitchen, dropping his wad of paper towels into the trash and tearing off a new batch from the roll.

"Finally," he said. "I can see a path to friendship."

As Waldo folded his new bandage, Dorothy saw Huana's shadow flash past the doorway. She was on the porch, settling under the window, exposed to anyone who might approach from the courtyard.

Dorothy raised the volume of her voice. "Intelligence, Mr. Wally. We don't need to be friends if we practice intelligence. I have a plan for both of us."

Waldo walked to the couch and sprawled under the window. "I'm listening," he said. "What's your plan."

"I read Mr. Lockjaw's helicopter manual. It has a tool called GPS. The GPS will tell you where Mr. Lockjaw and Willa found me. That is where you will find the Savant. Only the chief knows where to find the *Silver Book*. Mr. Sam can fly to get what he wants. He doesn't have to come back if you know what to do."

Waldo leaned forward, his good eye wide. "What do I need to do?"

"You need to tell him to take Shori, so she can speak a language they know. Before they leave, puncture the gas tank. Maybe they will make it there, maybe they will not. Certainly, they won't have enough gasoline to make it back. We can fly there together when they don't return."

"Hu Haw." Waldo whispered his peculiar shout of excitement, then went suddenly thoughtful. "I'll have to disable their gas gauge. I'll have to do something about their radio."

"Nobody listens where they will be going." Dorothy said. "If you keep your word, the *Silver Book* will be yours. The Savant will give you what you want if I go with you. Promise to let the Savant live in peace, and your club can use my DNA. After you get what you want, I know you can't let me live."

Dorothy stiffened as soon as she finished speaking. A bobbing head above the palmetto line let her know Sam was returning. "Hurry," she said loudly. "I see Mr. Sam is coming back. Deal?"

The sound of skittering footsteps on the porch, followed by the soft thud of Huana's feet hitting sand at the end of her leap over the rail gave Dorothy a moment's worry, but Waldo didn't notice. From the steady stride of Sam, walking into the courtyard, she guessed Huana was able to get away unseen.

"One more thing," Waldo said. He laid his bandage on the couch and picked up the nutcracker. "I have to make this look convincing."

51

S AM LIFTED HIS HEAD when screams of pain came from the guesthouse and picked up his pace. When he reached the stairs, Waldo stood in the doorway to greet him, one hand pressing paper towels to his face, the other stretched, palm up. One whole tooth and shards from another lay in his hand.

"How'd it go?" Sam asked.

"It was like pulling teeth. The Savant, the book, it's all there. Did you get the GPS?"

Sam held his palm up and displayed the device.

"You need to take Shori. She can speak the language." Waldo glanced over his shoulder toward the lounger. "Bring me back the chief, and a young pretty one," he added. "We're done with this bitch."

"Shori will be happy." Sam peeked into the guesthouse then pushed Waldo backward, barging into the room. "I told you to keep her alive for Shori."

"Relax, boss, she's fainted. I need a little dose of pain relief myself." Waldo opened his suitcase and removed a brown plastic bottle, dumped a pile of pills into his hand and swallowed them without water.

"I don't know how you do that," Sam remarked. "You're a freak."

"No water in the fridge, boss. The well water sucks."

52

A BOX OF SORROW

Because our portals to the outside world were shut, we missed the final act of Dorothy's nine decades in the short life. Her war was over. The end came while the *Killer Bees* negotiated the final mix of the songs on the album.

I was attempting one final time to mask our weariness with *Bingle Bells* by speeding up the recording, trying to engineer some cheerfulness into our performance with a quicker tempo. Knowing Robert's history, I should have known better.

I guess it's true. Timing is everything. We were unaware Kae'Lairy put Dorothy in the box, until she spoke. When she spoke, she said the worst thing possible.

Kae'Lairy ushered Dorothy into the box without his usual, "I am the mighty Kae'Lairy" speech. He didn't show her the courtesy of informing her where she was. He didn't include us in witnessing Dorothy's final moments the same way I was shown the happenings outside the box when Asitr and Robert were snared. She traversed the mental distance between the panic of drowning, to the ecstasy of the dopamine hallucinations, and then the final destination in reality without so much as a "be at peace".

Too late, I recognized my mistake in speeding up the recording. As soon as the song began to play and our voices lilted like the singing chipmunks. Robert's button may have gone unpressed, but who knows? It was the cheerful, innocent Dorothy who pushed the button so hard Robert shattered.

"Ooh," she warbled, "Is this the waiting room for Heaven? I didn't expect the angels to sing like Alvin and the Chipmunks."

"You tricked me. This is Hell," Bobby shouted. "I am not Alvin Chomuk. Baal Alayat, come to me."

What could anyone say? We couldn't reach out and touch him, we couldn't undo his memories. One more time, Bobby screamed the name of the devil he once trusted. Then with a scary, ferocious snarl, he addressed everyone in the box.

"You can all stay in Hell, I'm leaving."

Those were Bobby's last words. Even at the campfire on the moon, he was gone to us.

"Dammit," I swore.

"Come back," Asitr pleaded.

Dorothy's reaction showed how completely in the dark she was about what just happened.

"I sorry?" Her apology came as a question, followed by a timid, "Why am I in Hell?"

53

O TIS ROSE FROM HIS CHAIR and walked to the window. "Eighteen years go by."

Dr. Milton recognized an unusual tone in the way Otis spoke the words. He stood up and joined him at the window.

"May I?" he asked, nodding his head toward the marble. "Take your time."

Otis let the marble slip into the doctor's hand. "Poor Bobby …" He trailed off without following up.

Dr. Milton cleared his throat and broadened the focus. "I was thinking of the entire collection in the box."

"The collection," Otis repeated. "We were an odd bunch, weren't we?"

The doctor held the marble up to the light, turning it slowly, stopping when Jarvis entered the room.

"New patient, doctor. It's another John Doe." Jarvis stood silent, waiting for instructions. When none came, he nodded to Otis, dropped a clipboard onto the bed, and left the room.

Without commenting on the new patient, Dr. Milton leaned against the windowsill.

"Two of you never died, in the earthly way of thinking. You're traveling with your bodies in cryogenic storage. Two of you are clinically deceased, bodiless."

"True facts," Otis answered. "Any other observations?"

After a pause, Dr. Milton followed up. "I couldn't help but notice who wasn't snared into the box. I think I know why, but I'd like you to tell me. Why aren't Lock and Willa there with you?"

"You know the answer, Doc." Otis waggled his fingers, reaching both hands out for his marble, like a toddler taking back his security blanket. "We suspected it all along. After Dorothy arrived, and Asitr figured out who she was, we moved our suspicion from theory to accepted fact. We were in the box because we were humans who know how to speak in the language of the Adam."

"Yes." Dr. Milton handed Otis his marble and asked another question. "There's one more traveler with you, not human, but like you, a prisoner. Why doesn't Kae'Lairy take him to his judgment? Did Asitr dot his I's and cross his T's in the trial? Or is there something else?"

"There's always something else, Doc." Otis puffed a quick "hah," then sat back down in his chair. "We were just about to figure it out after Dorothy told us her story from Sam's island. The *quipu* information was revealing. We knew enough to ask the right questions. I was going to be the first kid in my box to solve the riddles."

Dr. Milton returned to his chair, faced Otis, pulled himself to the edge of his seat, and leaned his elbows atop his knees. "Thank God. I never thought we'd get to the answers. What did Asitr get out of the information? Did you guys get to the bottom of the 'unknown language' reference? The trinary math system, the three-layered balls, the different sized *beads* above the *quipu* on the golden calf. Did you solve all of it?"

Otis grinned like he was about to deliver the punchline of a bad joke. "We never asked her our questions. We went to sleep."

"You went to sleep?" The doctor sat back in his chair as if pushed. His posture was straight, his eyes sending signals of surprise and disappointment.

"Yep. For eighteen years. We dreamed, but we dreamed alone. Our ability to communicate was taken away. Eighteen years of dreaming is a long, long time."

Upon realizing answers weren't going to fall in his lap, Dr. Milton relaxed into his listening position and waited for Otis to continue.

"We woke up on the moon." Otis squirmed a little in his chair. "Baal Alayat was unfettered and no longer silenced. The windows opened again, and I could feel Kae'Lairy was carrying us toward the final scene of his breakdown, his last attempt to walk an ethical tightrope.

"The moon was like a dream, you know, how things just happen for seemingly no reason, but it doesn't surprise you? That aside, I knew this was real, and we humans were background actors sent on stage without a script.

"Watch and learn, kids." Alayat was the first to speak. His voice was confident, sinister, and greasy. It sent shivers through me.

Through the portal behind us a black sky, perforated by designs set in starlight, framed a thin haze around a way-blue planet. I felt challenged for words, but Dorothy summed it all up with just two.

"The world," she said reverently.

"You should have seen it before you turned her out to whore for you," Alayat said. "She's taken a lot of abuse from your kind."

Kae'Lairy's voice jolted me back to the view of the campfire. "I have in mind the difference between angels and Human," he said. With that, the dance began.

I sensed him before I saw him. When Kae'Lairy sat and placed his box on the ground, I saw him take form. "Look," I said.

"I see him," Asitr answered.

Dorothy whispered, "Oh, my."

Alayat asked, "See who?"

Our new arrival glowed, and I knew he was giving me a gift. When his glow went dark, I understood the poses, tells, and rules of the dance. Everything that nuanced the words spoken by the angels was clear to me.

None of the angels reacted to his presence. I understood why. A *Big Wing*, higher in rank than Kae'Lairy, showed up for Kae'Lairy's moment of decision, and he masked his presence.

This new witness waited patiently for Kae'Lairy to explain his predicament. Listen to the recording. This, finally, is where Kae'Lairy tried, in a tortured soliloquy, to justify his actions, keep a secret, and define the two options he weighed without resolve. Listen.

54

KAE'LAIRY'S PLEA

B ROTHERS, I HAVE MORE IN MIND than differences between species. I'm thinking of the throne.

God built his throne on the largest source of energy in the universe. He chose to harness its power to fuel the creation locked in his imagination.

Explosively, he focused a release of energy to force the simple to become complex then joined the complex into the composite materials needed for building what he imagined.

Every creation requires energy, and all energy is waiting for inspiration or imagination to give it direction. I'm not saying he needed that location to found Heaven. He could have chosen to create something less enduring.

God chose this reality. Through the eons of imagining, measuring, and building what could be sustained, he has protected it jealously. He trusts the throne to last forever in the same way we trust his creation to endure.

If a lesser mind were to control the throne, we would have a world without good endings or no world at all. The thin rings of Saturn would scatter into random dust particles, the Milky Way would spill into chaos, the firmaments would rush to fill the vacuum of space.

I, Kae'Lairy, was among the throng, created to protect the throne. How could I do any other thing? No other thing is so important. Why else would I have my abilities?

Clarity was confounded on the day the Lord revealed the wall of humans in the throne room. When I first saw it, it appeared spotlessly white. When told there were one-dimensional illustrations of human souls moving across the wall, I doubted my eyes. Each illustration, I was told, depicted a human being, scrolling in sync with the measurement of time.

Although endowed with full knowledge of the numbers ruling the three-dimensional world, I was unable to visualize the movement of invisible dots on a white surface.

On the night God gave human souls a portion of his spirit, I saw colors begin to radiate and move across the wall in tandem with the passage of time. Each soul remained invisible, but each soul's spirit came alive in colors. Their inspiration and imagination added tone. Choices each soul made added energy. The energy expended in creating from imagining and inspiration added brightness to each color. A phosphorescent haze of blending hues gave the appearance of breathing in and out, as each soul interacted with its new spirit, and the spirit shared inspiration and creation with other souls.

Seeing the evidence of moving light, I accepted the invisible one-dimensional world. The moment I accepted the concept, I was gifted with the ability to see seven additional primary colors.

As men did what he willed to do, some blends of my new colors breathed out ugly hues onto the tapestry. As others resisted the temptation to forget they are the egg and not the chicken, their radiance beautified the wall.

I saw beauty in the lights, and was enlightened in its beauty. This peculiar artwork, this self-creating monument to God's perplexing mandate for sentient creatures with free will … How could anyone consider turning out the lights in such a tapestry?

I considered doing that very thing. I was born to protect the throne. Yet, I wasn't born to remove from God's sight so unique a creation.

Given the threat I saw to the throne and the crime I would commit in erasing God's tapestry, I had no option but to find a third option.

I gathered those who were an immediate threat and resolved to wander, shunned for eternity, rather than deliver the dangerous to their appointments before the throne.

Woe that my shade of hoobida was not the answer. More and more, as I wander, I feel the temptation to fall.

Now, I know what I must do. If Heaven has a wall, glowing with the light of angels, my color will be putrid. Is a putrid life better than a shunned life? Woe to anyone who must decide. Woe to me, I have decided to color myself putrid.

Inside my box, there is a fallen demon, late for judgment.

I have a crippled innocent, cruelly warped and unable to repair himself.

I have a spirit with the protection of Heaven, terminally human, yet sincere.

I have a spirit, delightful for her attitude of a child, overripe for her rewards.

I have a spirit who has read the same secret of my own undoing.

I've judged only one to be free of the knowledge that could usurp the Lord from his throne. I've protected her by silencing all of them with the gift of sleep. Today, I commend her spirit to you for delivery to the Lord.

The rest of us are earthbound. There, we will remain together, entombed in a golden prison until the Lord, should it be in his will, returns to earth and makes things right.

55

O TIS STARED AT HIS SHOES after silencing the soliloquy and whispered, "I'm the guy who read too much."

Dr. Milton stiffened, setting both his feet on the ground, and spread his arms. "But, obviously, that didn't happen."

"No, doc. Thanks to some simple two-step dancing of big wings."

Doctor Milton jumped to his feet, picked up the clipboard from the bed, and walked to the door. "That will have to wait," he said. "I have an incoming patient to attend to. Walk with me. Say goodbye to your pigeon; we won't be returning to the room."

"There isn't much left to tell. How far are we going to walk?"

The doctor motioned with his head toward the hallway and retrieved his recorder from the pill cart. "Don't say anything until we get our buggy."

Otis stood at the window for a moment without moving. Doctor Milton stopped at the door and turned toward him. "Well?" he asked. Then he walked into the hallway without waiting for an answer.

Otis followed.

On the way to the nurse's station, Dr. Milton scribbled on the forms attached to his clipboard. Up ahead, a gaggle of personnel heard their steps approaching. All but Rishard and Jarvis scattered before they made it to the desk.

On arrival, Dr. Milton handed Nurse Rishard the clipboard and stepped behind the desk. "I need to use the computer," he said, adding, "Jarvis, would you escort Mr. Beckley and me to the Sylvan building? I'm arranging a buggy."

Jarvis didn't answer immediately, he looked sideways at Rishard then cut his eyes to Otis, and then back to Rishard.

"Uhh ... Nurse wants I should get the John Doe room ready. Want I should do which thing first?"

Neither one answered the aide. Nurse Rishard shuffled through the papers on the clipboard and asked, "Did you get the room number right, Doctor?"

"It's empty, right?"

"Yes."

"Then the room number is correct. Please check my printout for more instructions." Dr. Milton pressed the button on the printer and stood up from the chair. "These are instructions for the staff. I'm assigning Jarvis to his room."

Before the nurse could read the instructions, Dr. Milton asked Jarvis, "Well? Are you free to accompany me?"

Jarvis looked at Rishard for the answer and she was slow to reply, still focused on reading the doctor's new orders for the incoming John Doe. "You want ... You want the staff to call the John Doe 'Bobby'?" she asked.

Otis put one hand over his mouth to cover a wide grin and squeezed the marble with his other.

Jarvis scratched his head vigorously. "Nurse?"

"Yes?" she asked absentmindedly, before catching up to the doctor's question for Jarvis. "Oh ... yes, sure, I can get Mayfield to cover for you."

"Jarvis won't be returning, Ms. Rishard, Tell Mayfield he's all yours, indefinitely."

"Let's buggy up, Doc." Jarvis grinned like a kid out of school for the summer.

"First, to my office," the doctor blurted. "Then we go buggy."

Dr. Milton was already fast-walking to the elevator, forcing Otis and Jarvis to hop-step in an effort to catch up.

As the door closed, and the elevator dinged, Rishard read the last line of the doctor's instructions.

"Freakin' what?" she asked herself out loud. "Notify IT to scrub *The Chipmunks* songs from the Christmas playlist? Wait 'til Dr. Abrams gets back."

56

D R. MILTON MOVED BRISKLY PAST HIS SECRETARY on the way to his office. "Budget forms for Friday," he said. "Jarvis gave me your note about the tickets. Thank you."

Jarvis followed behind, keeping in stride, and tipped an imaginary cap toward the secretary. "Good morning, Ms. Mottert. You look beautiful today."

"As opposed to yesterday?" she asked, without taking her eyes off the computer screen.

Otis followed behind them, pulled along by the wake of the two energized men, and smiled toward Ms. Mottert as he passed her desk. The secretary glanced at him and returned the smile without interrupting her flying fingers on the keyboard.

Inside the doctor's office, Otis waited by the door and took in the pictures on the walls. The expected diplomas and certificates were there, but mostly it was wife, mother, father, 1960 Chevy convertible, and a group picture of soldiers posing in a desert. One framed art print hung by the door, sure to be seen each time the doctor left his office. It was *The Scream* — Edward Munch's famous self-portrait of the moment he was terrified by a sunset.

Jarvis went straight to the window and rocked heel to toe while he watched the activities on the campus below.

"Man, that deer can jump," he said to nobody in particular, "Ol' Fosdick scared him up out the meadow."

Dr. Milton looked up from the briefcase on his desk. "Fearless is in the meadow?"

"Cuttin' the hell out of those weeds, Doc."

"Catch up to him, please. Tell him to meet us at the Sylvan building." Dr. Milton continued removing papers from his briefcase and placing them in a folder. "Thanks Jarvis," he said, as his aide walked out the door. "And secure the buggy, please. We'll meet you downstairs."

After Jarvis shut the door, the doctor closed his briefcase and pulled a glossy brochure from the papers he'd sorted into the folder.

"I was afraid I'd left this in my shirt pocket yesterday," he said." He peeled a yellow Post-It note off the back of the brochure and held it up for Otis to see. "You're going to need this," he said. "Now, tell me about that big-wing two-step."

"Don't bother curling up in your listening pose, Doc," Otis began, "This didn't take but a few minutes to get settled."

He walked to the window, and stared at the meadow below him before telling the doctor what happened.

57

THE LESS THAN A MINUTE WALTZ

I THINK IT'S BEYOND SAFE TO SAY humans can't match the mental reflexes of angels. None of us processed the moving parts of Kae'Lairy's soliloquy, the path to Heaven for Dorothy, or his decision to sentence the rest of us to be imprisoned in a golden tomb as quickly as Alayat.

Alayat reacted strongly to the words before we had a chance to weigh them. The box filled with a wail that cut like a guillotine, but it registered, to me, as no more than a startle response. Bobby and I, the two living humans, were outside the box as quickly as a severed head drops into a basket. I was at peace inside the light of the angel who stealthily witnessed at the campfire. Inside the box, however, something very powerful was happening. The box rattled.

Within the glow that calmed us, a voice commanded, "Be at peace."

The rattling of the box continued, but as the glow dimmed, I saw the crouching bows of submission from Jederic, Barabajyl, and Kae'Lairy.

The new angel picked up Kae'Lairy's box in one hand and ended the rattling with a promise. "When you calm yourself, I will deliver you to the throne."

After speaking the words, he pointed a finger toward Kae'Lairy. "Never has a bondsman been imprisoned in his own box. You have no choice but to enter now. I invite you to enter on your own, but don't consider believing in the possibility of options. Enter, and surrender your orb.

Kae'Lairy sprang from his bow of submission into a threatening posture. Jederic and Barabajyl moved just as quickly and placed their bodies between us and the two dangerous angels.

The pulsing threat of power from Kae'Lairy was a stark contrast to the posture of the angel he threatened, whose posture didn't change. He spoke as if unconcerned. "I offer you the option I once gave a mule. The gate is open. You can take the Carmelita solution and, God willing, return to us, but walk through the gate you must. Enter the box."

He held a blue orb toward Kae'Lairy. He said, "From dissipated body, to new, with all my memories from the storage on this orb, I've returned, empowered, and instructed by the Lord."

"Olphrenjii!" Kae'Lairy's shout was a burst of joy. As fast as the name left his mouth, he was gone, trailed by a stream of blue light, into the box.

In the mud of my mind, where I tried to slog through those seconds of dancing, it took a while to realize I had taken form, like a weak holographic image. No longer in view, were Alayat, Asitr, Dorothy, Kae'Lairy, Olphrenjii, or the box. I saw Bobby on the ground, an ethereal form, curled in the fetal position. Catching my attention with a high octave hum, Kae'Lairy's marble spun between my feet.

"Pick it up," Barabajyl said. "It knows where to go."

I lifted the blue marble and the humming stopped. "Tell me what's happening," I pleaded.

"We should sing until we know," Jederic said, picking up his guitar.

Sing? Nothing made sense. Where was the clarity I expected? I missed the safety of the box. "One small step for man?" I asked, rhetorically. "This drab no-man's land," I ranted, "covered in dust, pockmarks, and rocks, plastered in wallpaper with an image of mother earth is one small step for man into a demented hell of angel secrets and mind rapes."

I spun in a circle to take in the full landscape and stopped when I returned to the view of angels by campfire light. Barabajyl took a step toward me and lifted his eyes. I knew what was coming but I stopped him. "Don't give me that *be-at-peace* booshwa. Tell me what's happening."

"Don't discourage the lad," Barabajyl answered, while pointing at Robert. "He's fragile."

"Can we agree to a pact, the three of us?" Jederic offered. "At the campfire we can't agree to answer your questions. It would cross a line and interfere with your own requirement to find answers. Besides, we would be guessing."

My spirit was trembling like a baby deer, caught between two lions. "I'm afraid to commit to a pact," I answered. "I don't know your intentions."

Jederic picked his guitar off the ground and sat next to the fire, shaking his head.

Barabajyl struck a pose of impatience. "Of course you can't say. You haven't even heard the proposal. Sheesh Kamushka, friend. We need your permission to propose a pact.

"I'll listen," I promised.

Barabajyl sat next to Jederic and made his proposal. "I propose we each give our best guess about what is happening, keeping in mind, guesses aren't facts and opinions aren't truth. One round of guessing, no questions, then we sing away the time it takes for the business in Heaven to finish"

"Will Olphrenjii return for us?"

"That sounds like a question," Barabajyl said. "Did you leave your brain in the box?"

"I think the rings of Saturn are safe," Jederic interjected. "Take that as my one opinion, should you agree to the limited pact.

I agreed to the pact with yet another question. "Who goes first?" Realizing my question already overlooked Jederic's offering, I wondered if, indeed, I had left my brain in the box.

Jederic ran his fingers across the guitar strings and insinuated an almost familiar memory from the musical period of romantic optimism following the second world-war. "I've already gone first," he said. "What opinion do you want to share?"

I offered the composite view of the three travelers in the box, brainstorming, disagreeing, yet somehow, in hindsight, making sense to me in that moment. Nervously, I began meshing our three views together.

"I believe God would not lie." I fumbled for the right words to use next. The two angels waited patiently for me to finish. "He's created a conundrum, a loophole, by promises that leave him defenseless.

"I think, like the walls in Kae'Lairy's box, the throne is a device to harness the energy on which it's built. If you stand before the throne, and speak the proper command, with the proper language, you can direct its function. Alayat has manipulated God's promises in order to stand before the throne.

"I've read portions of Baal Zebub's book of sciences. His writings are laid out like a puzzle. To read it thoroughly, you need to ask for specific information. I immersed myself in questions about weaponry. I'm unfamiliar with what it says about the science of time, but I know he has a chapter dedicated to the concept. One sub-chapter is listed under the heading, *Travel*. If Alayat knows the science of that chapter, or Kae'Lairy understands it, either of them could wound God in his Achilles heel through the manipulation of time travel."

I ended my speculation and waited for Barabajyl to speak. His long stare in my direction made me wonder if he expected me to say more. I added, "Time will tell."

I believe he wanted me to acknowledge I knew I could be wrong. He gave his opinion after I declared that possibility.

"God doesn't do fanciful, wishful thinking. Don't challenge him to find a rock too big for him to lift. He deals only in the possible. The only way to travel in time is with memory. Memory can't reach past now, because now is in the past as quickly as it's recognized. The path to travel ahead of time is a rock too big to lift. We know the fallen want to control the throne, but to believe it has the power to change the fact of time is fanciful, wishful thinking, tempting the dreamers of fiction and the mighty who forget the limitations of possibility."

We all honored our pledge for no follow-up questions, and marked the passage of time with song until Olphrenjii returned.

When Olphrenjii returned, he repeated the words Enoch said to Asitr when the meetings between fallen and human were concluded. "No questions." By then, I expected it.

In my farewell to Jederic and Barabajyl, I told them how much I enjoyed my newfound skills at three-part harmony. They grinned, posing the meaning of the southern expression, *"Bless your heart."* Jederic diplomatically added, "We enjoyed your joy in participation."

*   *   *

My next recollection was lying on concrete, shivering, marble in hand, and unable to speak until a "match made in Heaven" asked me why I was here. Getting around to answering your question, Doc, I'd say, I'm here to stumble onto mysteries, accept most answers will elude me, and be thankful for the ride.

58

THE SYLVAN BUILDING

O N THE BUGGY DRIVE ACROSS CAMPUS to the Sylvan building, Dr. Milton and Jarvis introduced Otis to changes he could expect when he ventured out into the world. The buggy was one technological change they pointed to. "Tell it where you want to go and relax," the doctor told him, "it's self-driving."

"Long as the batteries don't go south on ya," Jarvis added.

"You'll see a lot of those cars on the street — taxis mostly — using the same technology, but be aware," Dr. Milton warned. "For the most part, the wild neighborhoods aren't accessible through the program. It's a safety issue. Lately, however, the system has shown a vulnerability to hacking. If you get hacked to an unexpected location, give up your ETM card without a fight. It's safer."

Jarvis again added a punctuation to the statement. "People are gonna eat. Don't judge 'til you get a look at what we've voted for these days."

With that chilling set of statements spoken, the buggy stopped in front of the Sylvan, and the doctor and his aide hopped out.

Otis lingered, eyebrows knit, rubbing his marble. Suddenly the buggy jumped forward, maneuvered in a circle, then crisscrossed the road in a series of figure-eights, before stopping again in front of the two astonished men. "It was only a guess guys, an intuition. This round blue puppy has more goin' for it than meets the eye."

"Just like that Steven Hawkman's wheelchair, I'll say," Jarvis sputtered.

"Hawkings," Dr. Milton corrected.

"I think I'll do fine in the world guys." Otis jumped out of the buggy, grinning. "I'm ready."

"Fair enough," Dr. Milton said. "I promised you a couple of things, Otis. One of them was to show you the man who made me doubt God."

Jarvis pulled his lips back in a grimace and groaned. He looked at his shoes but pointed to the top of the old brick building. "I ain't never goin' in that room again," he said. "That miserable man is cursed for sure."

"No need for that, we don't have access anyway." The doctor put his arm on Otis's shoulder, turned him to the door, and started walking. "I'll explain on the way to Bobby's room."

The three men entered the elevator and Jarvis pushed the button for the third floor.

"Fourth floor too, please," Dr. Milton requested. "Jarvis, you can go to Bobby's room and wait. Make a list of the staff you want to work with. If you see Fosdick, escort him up to the room. Mr. Beckley and I won't be more than a couple minutes."

Jarvis exited on the third floor and turned to Otis with two fingers pinching his nose. "Be ready," he said, "that stink is going to get to you."

When the door closed, Otis looked at Dr. Milton with one eyebrow raised and his mouth pinched. The lines between his eyes pushed together. He was asking a question that didn't need words.

"The stink isn't so bad in the hallway. We won't go into his room." Dr. Milton leaned against the elevator wall, watching the doors close, then continued. "Before he arrived, his patrons had devices installed to absorb most of the odor. Jarvis and I worked with his doctors during the transition. Jarvis was the only aide to stick with him. The others quit their jobs to avoid him. For the last eighteen years, he's had his own doctors and aides. His patrons pay a lot of money for the arrangement."

"What's all the ..." Otis began a question, but the elevator door opened, and the doctor shook his head and put a finger to his mouth while pressing the button to close the doors.

"If you have questions, ask now. The halls have ears." Dr. Milton pressed against the close-door button while Otis asked a series of questions.

"Why is he here? What does this have to do with me? How did he affect your faith?"

The answers came in reverse order of the questions. "This man never closes his eyes, even to sleep. The muscles around his eyes are perpetually tight, framing them with a hint of constant pain, or fear. Maybe both. When his hands are released from their restraints, he claws at his face and chest, gouging deeply enough to leave scars. Bathing him is a violent wrestling match. When fed, he will swallow his food, but self-destruction and eating are his only voluntary reactions to stimuli.

"I nearly lost faith after seeing the man try to pluck his eyeball from his head. I couldn't understand why God would allow that much self-destructive pain to go on in one man's solitary world

"What does it have to do with you? I'll let you answer that. I believe the people who brought him here did so because they want to know more about the only words he's uttered since he fell into his condition. *Silver Book*."

Otis dropped his jaw. Dr. Milton lifted his finger from the button. "The first door we pass is where their nurses monitor his vital signs."

The elevator door opened, and Milton stepped into the hallway, with Otis following. "The next door down is the air-scrubber, the third is the listening and monitoring station. He's under twenty-four-hour surveillance." The doctor's tone was that of a man giving a tour for a new employee. "And this room," he continued, "is where the patient lives."

Doctor Milton removed a form from the folder he carried and offered it to the man sitting in front of the patient's door. "Nothing new?" he asked.

"Same old." The man answered, while scribbling his initials at the bottom of the paper. "They're thinking they may need to take the other leg."

"Poor guy can't catch a break, eh?" Dr. Milton placed the initialed form back into his folder and added, "Dr. Abrams will be back in two weeks. He wants me to assist in any way we can."

"Not my call." The man at the door settled back into his chair and took a handkerchief from his shirt, placing it over his nose and inhaling deeply. A freshness, like the phantom odor of mountain air wafted briefly in the hallway. "They'll let you know if they need something."

On the way back to the elevator, Otis blew two strong breaths from his nose and whispered, "I need one of those handkerchiefs." When the elevator doors opened, he rushed inside and slapped at the button for the third floor. "That smell just festers. It gets more unbearable as it lingers. What is that?"

Dr. Milton exhaled into the hallway as the doors closed, then pulled the freshly signed form from the folder. "Dead flesh, rotting potato, sauerkraut farts, and the Auschwitz outhouses have been offered as guesses. You can get a sense of each. The man is rotting from the feet up, but it's a unique odor. Be glad you didn't get the full effect." He handed Otis the form and gave him his own opinion. "Look at the name of the patient. I call it the Waldo Kurtwood odor."

Otis stared at the name on the form. When the door opened on the third floor, he handed it back to the doctor without comment, and the two men stepped into the hallway.

"One less thing to think about?" Dr. Milton placed the paper back into his folder and removed the brochure he added while in his office.

"At least I had a concept for what to do about him." Otis shrugged. "Everything else is goals without plans, directions without maps.

Dr. Milton offered the brochure to Otis. "It's a vacation, booked and paid for. I had to cancel, but you really need to go. You might find your map there." He handed the glossy brochure to Otis and started walking toward Bobby's room.

Behind him, Otis pushed the button for the elevator and the doors dinged, opening immediately. The sound made Dr. Milton turn around. The two men stared across the distance until Otis spoke. "Thanks, Doc. You're right. I really have to go. First, I catch my ride, then I see Po. After that, I take a vacation." He stepped into the elevator, shouting as the door closed, "I'll be back to check on Bobby."

Dr. Milton walked back to the elevator. He watched the lighted numbers above the door as they traced the descent from three, to two, to one, then quickly, back up again. One, two, then three.

When the doors opened in front of him, Jarvis and Fosdick stepped out. "Did you see Otis?" Milton asked.

Jarvis answered, "Otis? No, what's up?

"I feel like I just lived through an old TV episode of *Quantum Leap,*" the doctor answered. "Let's get ready for our new John Doe. I have a plan. We need to get it done before Abrams returns."

ABOUT THE AUTHOR

Paul Moore was born in the Missouri Ozarks, raised in St. Louis, and eventually settled in the sand of central Florida. He calls each of these places home.

His inner mix of hillbilly river rat, lowlands daydreamer, sand road hermit, and reader of nineteenth-century history writers form the base of a non-elite education. These roots allow imagination to turn historic events into serendipitous thoughts. Those thoughts organize into stories, and stories become novels.

With the remedial help of a good critique group, and the birth of publishing companies that read a manuscript without asking first, "What are your credentials?", he's found a voice to share those stories.

YOU MIGHT ALSO ENJOY

RULES OF THE CAMPFIRE
BOOK ONE FROM STORIES IN GLASS
by Paul Moore

If you woke up one day and realized you had memories from more than seventy lives, fluid in every language you'd ever spoken, and recalled all the texts you'd ever read, would you wonder why?

Available from Water Dragon Publishing in
hardcover, trade paperback, and digital editions
waterdragonpublishing.com

www.ingramcontent.com/pod-product-compliance
Lightning Source LLC
Chambersburg PA
CBHW030138180626
46812CB00002B/749